Paul +
Enjoy!
sunsets warm
evenings! All the best

TOBACCO SUN

A novel

By Lorna Hollifield

For Annette Lovingood.

Mamaw, you taught me my ABCs, how to spell my name, and how to sound out the word "cat." I wouldn't be a writer if you hadn't provided the pen. Thanks for always telling me to "lay in there and grind." It turns out, I took the advice.

A FEW WORDS ABOUT TOBACCO SUN

"Dueling southern voices uncloak both the vengeance and virtue of family in a tender tale that will flood the hearts of every reader."

-**Mary Alice Monroe**, New York Times best-selling author of *Beach House for Rent*

"Debut author Lorna Hollifield crafted a thoughtful and challenging southern tale with both the beauty and darkness residing within the North Carolina tobacco fields and the deep complexities hiding within the unbreakable bond of sisters. Hollifield is a master with words, bringing the reader fully into a rural small town in a simpler time with its secrets, passions and longings just waiting for their day of bloom in the warm Tobacco Sun."

-**Dori Ann Dupré**, award winning author of *Scout's Honor*

PROLOGUE

The dry, sandy soil of the North Carolina foothills isn't good for much. It's a powdery, brownish kind of dirt that's awfully barren for such a humid climate. When the first European settlers made the trek across the coastal plain to discover the parched earth, they realized they'd starve if they didn't plant the food crops closer to the wet riverbanks. As for the miles and miles of unused sand hills, they would have to be reserved for the tobacco plants.

Tobacco...a strangely fragile, yet willful crop, desperate for survivorship, proved it could somehow adapt to the more arid ground in the state's wide middle. No matter the wars fought over top of its sprouts, or the roads built by its stomping grounds, some of the germ always managed to make it another season. Even when the 1940s rolled around, and the farmers had forsaken their precious fields to take up arms with men in rice pastures whom they'd never met, the plants were still born, deceased, and reincarnated like always. The perseverance of such crops might shine a nice light on the man who raised them and make those around him praise his farming techniques. He must have so carefully readied his field, implemented the best strategies, and employed the help of the brand new self-propelled combines to take on such a mighty task.

Surprisingly enough, just the opposite was actually true. Tobacco seeds aren't planted at all. The farmers don't scour the fields looking for the perfect womb where their precious crops can matriculate. There's no magical spot ready for them where they'll be cared for until flourishing into gorgeous green leaves. The tiny seeds are unceremoniously scattered out onto the earth where they scramble about trying to cling to any stable soil they can find. Some won't make it, but inevitably, some always do.

The lucky ones burrow into the ground to wait out the ebbing cool weather before the heat of the perfect summer day sweet talks them into sprouting. They then snake their ways through the mountains of manure masked as a powder to look like rich soil. They have to muster the nerve to stretch their heads up and find the light at just the right time, because they can only thrive with lots of sun.

If they make it that far, surviving frosts and flea beetles, they then get to fulfill their destinies, which starts with them getting cut off at the stalk. Plucked at their most beautiful, when the leaves beckon the plow, the survivors are harvested at long last. They are now chopped, sorted, and shipped away. At their new homes they get rolled into all kinds of different things; of different strengths, flavors, and sizes. From there, they wait.

TOBACCO SUN

They wait for the spark from a nicotine-hungry man to set them aflame, free them from the filter, and release them formlessly into the wind, scattered once again.

CHAPTER 1

SYDRA

Two policeman, one grasping me by each of my upper arms, led me not so gently into the drab room that smelled like sawdust. I looked around and saw no reason for this because everything in the sparse boxcar they were trying to pass off as a "conference room" was practically prehistoric. There was nothing new and fresh about it, and certainly nothing that inspired communication. However, I was about to have the conversation of my life, right here, in this stuffy, glorified cubicle with watermarks on the ceiling. I noticed a dented-in tin bucket in the corner, the kind used to milk cows. I guessed that was the out-of-shape officers' answer to the leaky roof. I could hardly wait for rain.

I assumed we were situated on the eastern end of the police station because the rising sun cut sharply through the sporadically missing blind slats. The stiff-jawed officers sat me down on a hard wooden chair that was bolted to the ground, and a little more forcefully than I cared for.

The pot-bellied officer said to the other, "Should we chain her waist too?"

"She's already cuffed," the other responded. "She can't weigh 110 pounds soakin' wet. I think the shrink can take her."

The bigger of the two cops nodded to the man who was already waiting for me on the far side of an ugly table ringed with coffee cup stains before they exited. I looked the man in his eye from the second I ambled into the room, but waited for him to speak to me. I wore the tiniest smug look on my face, if for no other reason, than to air my almost tangible confidence. I wanted him to feel it first.

The man leaned across the table extending his file-free hand, "Ms. Parramore, I'm Dr. Peter Garris. I'm with The University of Chapel Hill's Department of Criminal Psychology." He said this in a practiced monotone voice that bored me already.

I shook his hand, making sure to be the one to decide when to let go, while carefully keeping eye contact. I was impressed he had the balls to shake my hand so sternly. More often than not, men took my hand gently, only giving my fingers the slightest squeeze. They'd approach me in dimly lit rooms, hoping to celebrate my latest premier or magazine cover with me. The suitors would file in like union men reporting to duty, beckoned by my dress that was hemmed tighter at the knees than at the hips. It forced my hourglass figure to wiggle with every leading step I took, the perfect Glenn Miller song swaying the room to the rhythm of my own body. The two worked in tandem, pulling the bodies like magnets to the dance floor.

But first, the introduction. The men in the tailed tuxedos would spot me, whisper their typical names, and offer their hands. Palms facing the floor, they were always just too delicate for a self-respecting woman to take. It happened so frequently I'd developed a peeve about it; more than a peeve, a disgust. I was pleasantly surprised with Peter Garris' grip, however. At first glance, I was so sure he was a fragile shaker.

"Please tell me why you're here, Ms. Parramore," Dr. Garris asked me from my counterpoint, trying not to notice or care how beautiful I am...also trying not to care *who* I am.

I doubt he interviewed famous actresses on a daily basis. My guess is he spent almost everyday teaching the children of old money how to spot good candidates for lobotomies. He's never met someone like me. I'll use it to my advantage.

"You know why I'm here." I answered flatly, already feeling patronized.

"Yes, Ms. Parramore," his voice gave away nothing about him, "I need to know that you know the reason." He raised his eyebrows overtop of his thin silver-rimmed glasses.

"I know, ok," I answered with a quick grin. "Can we get on with it?"

"Humor me, Ms. Parramore. Please state your name, location, and reason you're here, as well as today's date." He sat cross-legged, dark brows still peaked, expectant of my compliance.

I rolled my eyes and sighed. "I'm Sydra Parramore.

I'm at the North Carolina Department of Corrections in Raleigh. It's June 29, 1947. You are here to evaluate me... *mentally*," I smirked.

    I knew what I was about to get into, and I was annoyed. I didn't know, however, if I was 100% ready to perform the little pony dance just yet, but the state was keying up the music anyway. I decided to let only a bit of my frustration out now, saving my poker face just a little longer. I knew I would need it. This was only the beginning. I was going to have to answer a lot of offensive and elementary questions by the time this was over. Time to grin and bear it.

    "Thank you," Dr. Garris said dryly.

    The man sitting across from me furrowed his newly wrinkled brow. I could tell he hadn't been middle-aged for long. I fixed my naturally half-shut marbled eyes on him, trying to decide exactly how old he might be. He'd just crossed that threshold and the decent looking man that once lived where he is now still lingered in his shadows. His hair was less than salt and pepper and his eyes deep brown, almost black. The shadow on his face, only a touch silver, seemed uncharacteristic of his professional demeanor. Someone like him is usually clean-shaven. Maybe the doctor *did* have a little flicker in him somewhere. Maybe this guy had some chops behind that stoic mouth.

    However, his tan buttoned sweater gave him away. Maybe they passed those sweaters out to all the Psych majors in school. Without the sweater, and the condescending attitude I could all but reach out and touch, he was fairly good looking. In another place, under different circumstances, with his income level, I would have flirted a little bit.

"Ms. Parramore," he cleared his throat seeming nervous for only a second, "I want you to tell me, simply, where it all started." He shrugged and turned his bottom lip down a touch. Forced ease.

"Where what in particular started, sir? You're going to have to be a lot more specific than that, *Doctor,*" I invited him to compete with my wits.

"I worded it that way, Ms. Parramore, because I want you to find your natural beginning. I want to get to the bottom of who you are, and how it relates to the... the situation at hand." He crossed his legs the other direction now, and smiled slightly.

I immediately noticed he'd avoided using the word *murder.* He didn't have a read on me yet, and didn't know if it was safe to bring it up. Good. I should keep him in that place. It shouldn't be his decision. Best he knows that now.

The doctor's body language had an air, especially the smile he'd just coerced. When I thought of how many more times I'd be forced to look at it, it irked me. I rolled my eyes so quickly it didn't even appear haughty, just hurried. I wanted this over with already, and I would have to deal with the psychologist's obviously high opinion of himself in the meantime. I hated having to play ball on the state's terms with these formalities... no, *evaluations.*

I took a deep breath and pursed my lips together, realizing I'd subconsciously made them pout. It's wired in me to do this, just like it's wired in me to sit with my shoulders uncomfortably far back. I'm conditioned to be alluring in every way possible. But, really, what could it hurt? He *is* a man. He has the exact same parts dangling between his legs all the other ones have. They're all the same, and since my recent successes in film, I'm starting to think I may be their queen.

I threw my hair, which was slightly less curly and less blonde than some of my Tinseltown rivals, behind my trim shoulder blade. This drew more attention to my C-cup cleavage, and sufficiently exposed my sleek collarbones. Even the dreadful orange ensemble I'd been given to wear couldn't hide my figure. It was just too noticeable, too uniquely perfect, to be masked by even the most drab drapery. I'm not necessarily cocky about it by choice, but because it's fact. I know what I look like, and my ego responds to it accordingly. Maybe I'd leave such opinions of myself out of any testimony.

"Whenever you'd like to begin, Ms. Parramore, please." Dr. Garris dropped the hint that he'd been patiently waiting on me to speak.

He wanted me to talk about the murder. He thought I'd just open right up with it at his go ahead. He wanted me to start with the man who died almost two months ago. He sat with a copy of my confession in his folder, but what he didn't know was why. He thought the answers were buried with the body, finally at rest now after weeks of investigations. The doctor thought I would begin by digging up the departed. He expected me to resurrect, first, what happened that day, to talk about how the hole got into the chest that was now decorated by a long, crude autopsy scar. However, he was wrong. The gun that shot the deceased had been cocked for years, and the hotshot doctor would have the version he needed soon enough. What he doesn't know is that the beginning isn't the page he's on.

I began in my fading southern accent, without knowing I'd spoken. "It started before I was born, I suppose...when my half-sister, Jimmi-Lyn, was born cursed."

CHAPTER 2

JIMMI-LYN

"You like that poster an awful lot, don't ya, Ma'am?" the bartender asked with a mouthful of marbles.

When he spoke to me I nervously pulled my pony-tailed hair down, letting the thick side of my part cover the side of my face. I didn't go out much, and was always nervous when strangers talked to me.

"Ma'am?" He bobbed about in front of me, trying to make eye contact.

I swirled the whiskey around in my smudged glass a little before my obligatory answer. "I don't know if it's like or love, sir...It may be something more like admiration and hate." I responded to the aging man while gazing up at the face on the wall, at the most familiar stranger I'd ever seen. I fought the urge to reach up and try to rub the rouge and lipstick right off of the paper, but I knew it wouldn't work. I felt like if I could, though, maybe I'd see the child's face that I'd been acquainted with so long ago. Maybe if I bobbed her hair and put a child's beret on her head, and cloaked her in a straight cotton dress, I'd really know her again for a second. Then maybe I could make a little sense of her. However, I knew it would take an act of magic to go back, and what she'd remain to me is what she'd always been...a beautiful little mystery in my life.

The woman in the poster was like a caterpillar; one of those bright green ones with blue horns. They're the ones always crawling up the sides of tree trunks, in my opinion, just to show off their own beauty. They've even been known to make the butterflies jealous. I'd trail after them as a kid, canning jar in hand, watching them, considering taking them as pets, contemplating how to catch them. Then I'd make the mistake of touching one without being able to help it, and I'd get stung. Still, I'd find another one, even more glorious, and think, surely something this gorgeous can't hurt me. But then that one would always sting me too. It seemed the more beautiful and vibrant the hue, the worse the burn. I wore all kinds of welts from the kisses of their spiny little bodies. But, fewer lessons are learned from welts than somebody might think. I never quit reaching for them.

The girl on the wall had been my biggest caterpillar, with the most potent of stings, and the most illusive of natures. Her face, so perfect, seemed out of place on the greasy wooden slat among the other random alcohol-inspired decor. Yet, at the same time, a place like this was where her face, body, or whatever she was showing off at any given time, seemed perfectly matched. Somehow it sat quite nicely next to the mounted rusty tricycle and road sign reading, "Possum Swaller Holler."

By photo alone, she seemed far too elegant for a po-dunk tavern on the bad side of town; but I knew more of her than her likeness on paper. Very little of what I knew were details about her private life, and I admittedly often wondered what was going on inside her pretty head. However, I'd always been aware that whatever it may be, was awfully rough around the edges. She had her own outskirts, and they fit in nicely here at Cahoots Tavern, positioned a little sideways overtop of a dirty ice box full of Schlitz beer. It's supposed to be refined, but just isn't. America's most distinguished beer, and Hollywood's most distinguished actress in Tobaccoville's most distinguished bar...it all made some kind of sense I couldn't explain, but could understand at least a little bit.

Though I felt I never truly identified with my sister, I knew the way about her. It's strange being so close and so far away from someone your entire life. It's kind of like watching a bird eat the seed you've put out for it. The bird will return to your windowsill everyday, and nests in your own front-yard tree. You'll memorize the variations of color in its densely feathered wings, and the unique hue of orange on the edge of its skinny beak. You'll give it a name, and even grow to love it on some level. But, you'll never touch it, never make a true friend of it. Then one day, as winter approaches, it'll simply fly away. I wasn't sure if my bird had flown away for good this time or not. I had no good tract record with birds or caterpillars.

I looked up at the picture again. She was still that girl to everyone here. Nobody had a clue what was going on. The press hadn't gotten a hold of it yet, though it'd been two months since the murder. Once the trial starts, though, there'll be no way to avoid it. Her public representative told the press Sydra was injured in a skiing accident while shooting a film in Switzerland opposite Clark Gable. The media was assured their favorite "it girl" was recovering comfortably at a European medical spa. Of course it had to be something glamorous. Always. I'm sure her fans are worried sick and she's sure to find a mailbox overflowing with well wishes if she makes it out on the other side of all this. Maybe it's better she doesn't find the gifts, though. She's reported people as stalkers for far less. Again, like that bird at the window, she enjoys being admired, not touched.

She's had plenty of admiration even with the ordeal. The police officers tried harder to help her keep her identity hidden than they did trying to find the Lindbergh baby. The Forsyth County police bent over backwards to make sure her stay was up to her liking. One would think she'd be filling out a comment card after leaving with the way they'd been falling all over her. She had private quarters, specially delivered meals, and unlimited access to the radio. They even let her have her own towels shipped in because the ones they provided were claimed to have chafed her.

County jail has been a cakewalk for her, but I knew things were about to be a lot different at the state capitol. It wasn't going to be playing rummy with the night guards from here on out; and I think I may have been feeling more stressed than she was about the situation. I'm still not sure if she's even considered this not going her way. Everything in her life has always seemed to magically work out somehow, and I'm not sure she's entertained the possibility that what she'd been charged with could be changing that for her. I can't tell if she's faking oblivion or if she's just that confident. For both our sakes, I pray it's confidence. I didn't know if I could handle her getting convicted.

The coming days would hold a lot for Sydra. Earlier today, she was transported about an hour and a half away to Raleigh from Winston-Salem to be evaluated by some big wig criminal psychologist from the college over in Chapel Hill. He'd determine if she's competent to stand trial, as well as if her intended plea will hold up in court. After that, I don't think the hush-hush is possible anymore. Trials are public. I may have dropped out of high school in the tenth grade, but I knew that much.

Government was one of the last classes I took before I dropped out. We had to memorize the preamble to the constitution, and then we studied the amendments. Number six was the right to a speedy and public trial. The teacher was an aging alcoholic known for dating all the widows in town. He had a crass sense of humor for an educator and gave us an inappropriate memory trick for each amendment. For the fateful number six, he reminded us that "six" sounds like "sex." He said the best sex is speedy and public. I don't know about all that, but I never forgot the amendment. But, because of that "public" part, we'll have to beat the news reporters off her with hired help before it's over.

The murder itself was so insignificant to the real

world, and in such a remote part of Tobaccoville, hardly anybody actually noticed it to begin with. The man who was murdered had left town going on half a decade before, and no one even knew he'd returned. Also, the day he died was the same day a nice young colored man from Connecticut started at first base for the Brooklyn Dodgers. Apparently a black man playing baseball was more scandalous than a murder, at least in North Carolina.

The nearest press was 45 minutes outside of town in Winston-Salem (where Sydra had been held until today). They reported an arrest had been made in a rural murder. The story was given about a paragraph on the lower right corner of the first page before being continued for an additional paragraph on page 3b. It was barely noticeable in the shadows of Jackie Robinson's smiling face, below the headline that read, "First Negro to slide into Major League Baseball." It would be it's own headline soon, though...if only those stupid reporters knew what they'd overlooked: "Sydra Parramore slaughters Hometown Hero." This was no squabble between two farmers gone wrong. This was Hollywood, and nobody knew a thing about it. To begin with, I don't think anyone outside family and neighbors knew Sydra was in town. But she'd been here alright, and charged with murder within 36 hours of her arrival.

"Oh, Sydra," I said out loud, still contemplating the gold-colored alcohol in my glass.

"You do love her, don't ya, missy," the bartender teased me using a strange tone.

"I do," I gave in, grinning sweetly in an attempt to remain pleasant.

"Well, you oughta make it a little less obvious," he moved in close to me, stale beer breath wafting, "I ain't judgin', but they don't take too kindly to that sorta thing in these parts." He smiled, showing me the time-worn yellow teeth that had been hiding behind his leathery skin.

I laughed instead of taking insult. "No, no...not anything like *that*. I just—I knew somebody like her once," I answered, avoiding eye contact with the man who was suddenly making me uncomfortable.

"Well, if you know somebody like Sydra Parramore I sure as hell wish you'd brought her with ya." His southern accent, jolly enough, grew a skeezy undertone, and I became aware that his plaid shirt unbuttoned to his pudgy navel.

"That's a popular wish, Sir, but she's much easier to pin up than she is to pin down." I tried to keep it casual, hoping he'd just stop talking.

He looked at me seriously and crossed his thick arms over his gut. "Ma'am, do you actually know Sydra Parramore?"

"Ahh...Parramore. No, no I don't know *her*," I answered and threw back the shot.

CHAPTER 3

SYDRA

"Jimmi-Lyn was born *cursed*?" Dr. Garris asked curiously.

"Absolutely," I responded, shaking my head as though it grieved me more than it probably did.

"Your sister, Jimmi-Lyn?" Dr. Garris glanced at his open file from shortly across the drafty room, then pulled a pen from the pocket of his shirt from underneath the ugly brown sweater.

"Half-sister... That's just the thing. She came from a man that might as well have marked her like cattle. She was, well, *doomed* I guess is a good word for it...even born with a jelly stain birthmark across the right side of her face. They let the doctor look at it a time or two, but there wasn't anything they could do. She'd always try to hide it with her hair or some makeup - if she could afford any. It's pitiful, really. Some people call it a port wine birthmark, but the blotchy way it sits there looks more like splattered-out jelly to me. It goes from the apple of her cheek to just above her jawline." I traced it out on my unblemished face. "She had a shot at being pretty too...exquisite bone structure, not so different from mine and my mother's..." I drifted deeper into my thoughts, painting Jimmi-Lyn in my mind's eye.

Dr. Garris looked as though he were attempting to sketch what I was describing on the pad in his lap, though I don't know that he was. I knew he had to take extensive notes, but I started to feel bothered when he did. His authority scratched at my skin like a wool sweater. I was always cautioned not to trust these psychiatric types, anyway. They looked for excuses to put women in lunatic asylums for whatever reason they could find. I'm sure Garris here would love to see me in a straight jacket with my hair standing on end. I shivered a little bit when I thought of this, my eyes still peering towards his furiously moving hand.

I continued when he turned the pad over and pressed his lips together in a way that revealed faint dimples. "Just like I was, Jimmi-Lyn was born to be a nobody in Tobaccoville, North Carolina right before the thirties ruined even the people who'd been born with a chance. We were both raised on government cheese in a town with too much debt to pave a single road. Not so much like me, her Daddy was James Leonard Brawley, about the most pathetic man to ever darken the Forsyth County line. He wasn't good-looking but wasn't really *ugly* either. Jimmi-Lyn has his bright blue eyes and charcoalish hair. He's actually the reason her eyes are bluer than mine. My daddy's were more grey." I shook my head finding my way again, "Anyway, he was alright. The eyes carried him mostly, but his teeth were frightful. *Trust me*, I've seen the pictures. Truth be told, a lot of women

25

were just drawn to his big tattooed arms. He was a lot of trouble, but just barely decent enough on the eyes to make that trouble really appealing to preacher's daughters. He certainly got to at least one I know of."

"Your Mother?" Dr. Garris confirmed.

"Yeah, they got together right before the U.S. got pulled into The Great War. My mother was pregnant with Jimmi-Lyn when he first got deployed. He ended up getting dishonorably discharged from the Army in '17 for a reason nobody seems to know, or won't tell me about if they do. Different rumors about it circulated, most of them related to him being a coward one way or another. Some say he ran from an attack and others say he tried to desert his unit while everyone was asleep. I don't know. Either way, he was a runner at the roots. Eventually, he ran from his family too, leavin' nothing behind but maybe of few jars of bootlegged liquor."

"So, Jimmi-Lyn's father deserted your mother and her?" He asked a question, but was trying to connect it with the reason I'm in here.

"Like, I said, *eventually*. After he was through beating on my Mama enough, he took off. Everybody in town always said his bark was worse than his bite. But, I've seen a lot of his teeth marks on Mama and Jimmi-Lyn - an awful lot for a dog that doesn't bite." I raised my eyebrows knowingly, making sure to sound conversational. Being personable was key. I needed the doctor to have at least *some* fondness towards me to keep from getting strapped down and having my brains stirred up.

"Excuse me, Ms. Parramore," the doctor's even-toned voice interrupted me.

"Yeah?" I asked, a little annoyed at his intrusion.

"I have to ask how this is all relevant. Jimmi-Lyn's father, from what I understand, hasn't been seen or heard from for years." He seemed less confused and more like he felt I was wasting his time.

I leaned forward, my elbows sitting awkwardly on my knees thanks to my cuffed wrists. I looked him emphatically in the eye and answered in a lowered tone, "I hate to bore you, sir, but this part is maybe the most relevant of anything I have to say. This is the beginning of all the other beginnings. This is the part where Jimmi-Lyn and I were both born, no *predisposed,* to certain things - our entire family, both the common and separate relatives, too. Everything to do with her has to do with me, just like everything to do with me, well, sadly, has to do with her. She's four years older than me, so the beginning of my life starts years before I even took up space in my mama's frail womb. She matters, and her past matters because she was there first. Whatever it is that has caused me to be sitting in this chair across from you - whatever it was that triggered me to do... what I did...it starts with Jimmi-Lyn's birth and it ends with mine. Besides those fates, it's just all a matter of dreadful circumstance. But, you sir, asked me to start at the beginning. Didn't you?" I cocked my head sideways and smiled with only my eyes.

He stared at me for a moment before speaking almost cheerfully, robbing me of my grand moment. "Predisposed...interesting term. Let's go back to that." He fished for a specific catch, seeming to have ignored everything else I had said.

"Cursed. Her fat-head daddy cursed her, and I cursed her deeper when I drew my first breath," I responded, relaxing back into my unforgiving chair.

"You're saying your birth, your very existence cursed your sister...and that is somehow related to the reason you're here? I'm just trying to make sure I'm zeroed in on your thesis right now, Ms. Parramore." He faked looking puzzled instead of skeptical, which I knew he was.

"It's a big part of it," I responded pulling a smuggled cigarette out of my pocket. Normally, I would have unveiled it from a sexy clutch purse, placing it deliciously in between my polished red lips. Today, though, I pulled it from the stiff pocket of a hideous jumpsuit that looked like it had been washed in a Mississippi creek. However, my lips, painted or not, took the vice divinely. I stared the doctor in the eye when I lit up and took my first draw. I dared him to protest. He didn't, and I wasn't at all surprised. I could feel my mouth trying to fight an egotistical simper. I'm not sure if I succeeded or not.

"Let's continue, Miss Parramore." He ignored my challenge.

"If we must. If it matters," I said too casually, wanting him to see how cool and collected I was.

His eyebrows and nostrils took the same arched shape. "You realize an individual is dead - by your hands. You realize you've been charged with murder, Miss Parramore," his mouth rested in the open position.

"I do."

"Since I am the psychologist evaluating you, don't you think you should take our discussion a bit more seriously?" He threw his penned hand in the air a bit, and I thought he might chuckle. "Look, I'm not your run-of-the-mill shrink. I don't want to just tell them you're nuts or dangerous and be done with it. My colleagues think I'm ridiculous, but I care to get to know the patient. I'm going to get to the bottom of who you are, Ms. Parramore, but I need your help. I'd appreciate some sincere effort from you."

I leaned toward him once again, and this time ground my cigarette out on a file folder laying on the pitiful excuse for a table. I could feel my nostrils flare a bit to match his and considered saying something smart-ass, or at least clever, to re-claim my dominance. I didn't like being out of the driver's seat. But, as quickly as I thought this, I realized my only way back into that driver's seat was to do his dance for a few minutes more. I gathered myself and fell back into line. It wasn't somewhere I was used to standing.

I took a breath in and began weeding through the memories, not sure what he was after. I did know that whatever I said was important, but not in the ways most people in my place might think so. I could not come off too sane or too bent. I had to find that perfect sweet spot in between the two extremes. I had to find the special sauce they're looking for to get me to trial but keep me out of prison, and certainly out of a straight-jacket with a piece of dirty rubber between my teeth. I put a lot of money into the bridgework of these perfectly straight pearly whites. I'd just hate to ruin them.

I needed to be in charge to put this thing to bed, and I knew that. I had to go to trial to make it all go away. However, I also needed to show the jury I had a hell of a good reason for committing the crime, to begin with. I needed whatever powers at be to see in that fleeting moment when a trigger was pulled, and a man bled to death in seconds, that I had every by-God reason in the world to pull it. Then, I needed the jury to set me free, so I could go back to my perfect life far away from North Carolina.

It wouldn't be easy to get a cast of southern farmers with sharpened pitchforks on my side, but I knew I could. It needed to be quick, too. I had already signed a deal to make my fourth film, which was only three months pre-production. We'd be shooting in Palm Springs by early October, and I needed time to prep with this little inconvenience behind me. I didn't know exactly what he wanted to hear, though I was sure I could figure it out in time. I thought maybe I'd just *start* with truth, and go from there if need be. I'd get to know everything I needed to about Peter Garris while making him think it's him getting to know me.

I gave myself a second to drift in my thoughts and decided to go on about the way Jimmi-Lyn became my Achille's heel. The doctor would soon discover that she *is* my story, though he doesn't see the relevance now. I knew he needed to see the brokenness that was Jimmi-Lyn to identify with me more, but I didn't know how authentic it would feel when I said it. I didn't realize this would be the truest part. She really was my conscience, my fears, and my drive. I hoped that would serve me well during this process. Dr. Garris, the judge, the jurors...they may not be able to feel sorry for an actress, but I knew they'd feel sorry for her unfortunate sister left behind up to her ears in the tobacco fields. If this murder had something to do with her, I'd be freed.

"The better part of Jimmi-Lyn's childhood looked a lot like her face," I began. "It might have had lovely moments here and there, but was mostly marred by a big ol' stain. Her daddy stayed in and out of the army, and then jail, for most of Jimmi-Lyn's toddler years - nothing too crazy. It was mostly small-time robbery here, smackin' somebody up there, and more often than not, it was something to do with our mother. When he got out of lock-up the last time, he treated Jimmi-Lyn like she was a bastard, always accusing Mama of being out with other men while he was away...which, truth be told, she probably was."

"So, James Leonard didn't believe Jimmi-Lyn was his daughter?" Dr. Garris asked.

"Mama was terrified of being by herself and wore out the mattress making sure she wouldn't end up alone. She was pretty, you know, in the damaged kind of way, and used it to her advantage the only way she knew how. She got what she wanted, which was just to have *somebody*. She didn't have much of a Daddy herself. Don't get me wrong. He really was a good man in a way - a hard man, though. He was a sharecropper and a

Southern Baptist preacher at a tiny church on the edge
of town. He spent almost all his time preaching or farming, but as the hardworking and God-fearing too often
do, tended to neglect his own family. He wasn't a terribly affectionate man but meant well enough.

My mama had no brothers either. She just wanted a
man to love her, fuss over her, let her wear makeup, and
not just be there to reprimand and judge her. She thought
a man telling her she was pretty was love enough. Somebody was always there with the right words, willing to
be her knight in shining armor for short-lived moments
in between James Leonard's reappearances...that's what
Jimmi-Lyn says, anyway. She has such a great memory,
better than mine. Everything goes way back with her."
I paused, trawling for something that I felt was almost
there, but left too quickly to come out of my mouth.

"Go on," Dr. Garris nodded, still sitting in front of me,
perched in pretension, his brown argyle socks showing.

"Whatever else she was, oddly enough, my mother
was loyal deep down." I recognized my slight defense
of her as I spoke, which shocked me. "Her allegiance
was only to James Leonard when he was there, but
when he was up the river, she scrambled like a squirrel
in the road. She didn't know which way to go...I think
she always just wanted to feel safe again. She'd try to
keep busy taking care of Jimmi-Lyn, or trying new corn-
bread recipes, but she'd get restless. She'd find whoever
she needed to find to feel however she needed to feel.
Jimmi-Lyn was his though, no doubt in the world. She
has his namesake and wears his face —well, minus the

birthmark. But it didn't matter. James Leonard Brawley had no qualms about tellin' Jimmi-Lyn exactly how he felt about her and Mama both. Truthfully, I think he didn't claim Jimmi-Lyn just because she was marked. He didn't want an imperfect child that caused whispers, stares, and other children asking rude questions. He didn't attempt to love her, or our mother, for too long. Finally, one day he got drunk, beat on both of 'em, and left. Mama, in that pathetic nature of her's, was on the prowl, and married my daddy six months later. I came about five months after they wed and finished off Jimmi-Lyn's chance at normalcy."

"Ms. Parramore," the doctor raised his hand to pause me, "why do you take responsibility for Jimmi-Lyn's fate? I don't know what her life is like, but if it's bad, it sounds like a lot of the issues stem back to her own beginnings. Why, in your opinion, do you believe your birth decided that her life would be no good? Do you think your existence can actually affect someone else to such a serious degree?"

"I'm beautiful," I answered quickly and expressionlessly.

"I am aware of who you are, Ms. Parramore," he replied directly, and perhaps proudly. "Your picture hung in many barracks during the war. I'd be lying if I said I hadn't watched all of your films." He caught himself before finishing. "Is it fame you feel cursed your sister? Perhaps, you're guilty that your looks made your life better than hers? Perhaps you're guilty that you were gifted with the tools that would eventually lead to your success?"

"Guilt? In part...maybe. But it isn't because my life is better, or *was* up until now at least. She was always treated as though mine would be, by nature. I would be the perfect one, and she would not. Strange...I never thought I really gave much of a damn until recently. I was happy just to be the blessed one and let her be the tragic one." I accidentally laughed out loud. "Who knew I'd fret so much about it now?" I shrugged playfully, turning my mouth down and lifting my eyebrows.

Dr. Garris twitched his upper lip slightly and scribbled something on his notepad when I spoke. Perhaps I revealed something, but I was unaware of it if I had. I needed to be careful of that - the Hollywood in me shining too brightly. I needed to stick to my plan and only show what needed to be seen. Maybe I'd just made myself seem too cold. I consciously softened my facial expression while I thought about it, remembering he needed to see my sympathy for Jimmi-Lyn above all else. This was just another role where I had to play the part and make it believable. I've proven I can do that on screen. I could do it here just as well.

"Let's talk about your childhood for a moment, Ms. Parramore," he said shifting gears. He was constantly trying to redirect me. He thought whatever he needed to break out of me would come from catching me off guard. This probably worked with most people. However I was anything but common.

I could tell he was considering that I might be a narcissist, and I'd have to ease him off of it. He was under the impression that I think so highly of myself, that I'm a curse to the world. That's not what I'd meant, but secretly I wondered if that's what I was. Whatever the answer to that question, I was still certain I was one to Jimmi-Lyn - a horrible curse.

I should be careful of him fancying me a narcissist, though. That kind of psychosis would not fare well for me. Narcissists go to prison because they don't get better. They're considered calculating and manipulative. I needed him to see a girl pushed to the edge for one brief moment of lunacy, and then make sure he tells it to the deciders of my fate on my behalf. To do this, I had to follow Dr. Garris' rules. I had to keep reminding myself of that, eye on the prize.

"Ms. Parramore," he said my name again, and I realized I'd zoned out.

"I'm sorry. I was thinking." I gave him small a closed-mouth smile.

"Quite alright, Ms. Parramore. As I was saying, can we speak about your family now? As much as Jimmi-Lyn's background has fascinated me, it's important I learn more about yours at this point."

"You want to talk about my father," I sighed.

"Start wherever you like, but make it about *you*," I could tell he felt as though he were beginning to budge me.

Good. He feels in control again.

"Alright," I answered lighting the third cigarette I'd smoked, "let's chat about Sid."

CHAPTER 4

JIMMI-LYN

$\mathcal{S}$omething started doing the backstroke in my head after I took the second shot. I'd only drank a handful of times in my life, and I might fit the stature of the average 12-year-old boy. The shots I'd taken were running amok inside of me and I didn't know how to calm them down. I'd never been a popular kid, so I never learned to drink. I wasn't invited to bonfires after home team wins, or parties after the school dance like the normal teenagers. I think it's in these early social rituals where they figure these things out. I guess I should have learned to be social, too.

I remember Sydra pulling the crinoline out from underneath her powder pink prom dress in the parking lot of the high school before turning up a bottle of Old Crow. Her date hadn't even gotten his car started, and the principal was standing no more than 15 feet from her, but she didn't care. She had so much life about her. I was supposed to pick her up and bring her home for exactly that reason. But instead, I watched her throw her head back cackling, sitting on top of the back seat of the convertible Oldsmobile as it took off, packed full of laughing kids, all rearing to tie one on. I remember her blonde hair hanging in curls just below her bare shoulders, blowing in the wind, seeming to sway to the Billie Holliday tune coming out of the muffled speakers. I don't know that I ever wanted to be her more than right then.

The closest I'd come to a night like that was when I was somewhere around 17ish. I'd trotted out by the barn by myself with the plan of getting drunk off the moonshine I'd swiped from the glove box of my step-father's truck. I didn't even get one shot down before I was coughing everywhere and shaking off the chills it gave me when it hit my throat. I checked my mouth with a flashlight to be sure my tonsils weren't on fire when I got back to the house. It wasn't exactly a romantic moment.

A year and a half later I had some wine my 74-year-old neighbor conjured up in his basement with used field piping. I tried to like it two or three times, but I just couldn't. Smacking my lips together and letting out a lying *ahhh* wasn't enough. The stuff tasted like a rotten grape that had been doused with ether, and the harsh liquid made my legs tingle after four sips. It was never more than a glass at a time - if it was even that much. I forced it down to try to feel more like an adult, but it didn't do the trick. That was about the extent of my drinking experience until today.

Needless to say, I wasn't used to straight whiskey, and it certainly wasn't helping take my mind off of anything. I don't know why the winos in town always looked so happy. I'd always heard that the perfect fermented grain could numb even the heaviest problems, but right now I'm not buying it. The footage is still playing, over and over, just like always. The whiskey wasn't erasing the hours of film I had on reserve, and I didn't know what would. I felt like I was sitting in a dark, empty room all the time, watching a homemade film. It always started like any other slide, with smiling faces, children running, and food being served. My movie just had a really sinister ending; one that I kept hoping would change if I watched again.

However, it never did. I always ended up there with Sydra the day of the murder, and it haunted me every waking second. I'd seen everything, and I knew all the awful details. The death itself never leaves me; that actual moment when the life was gone from the body lingers. It's there with me all the time now, no matter where I am, or how happy everyone else seems to be. Nothing and no one can seem to drive it out. It isn't smothered by the humidity or hushed by the buzzing insects. The clamorous and thick summer itself cannot hide it for even a moment.

I'm not haunted by the person who died, but by the image of the actual death. A ghost would almost be better to contend with. At least I could argue with him, say things to him, encourage him to leave, pray him away maybe. Instead, I'm left with the image of this quiet, inanimate thing that always has to be carried. It's the heaviest picture known to man, and I am its handler. I think it weighs 300 pounds and spends most of its time sitting just north of my belly button, though it's been known to vacation in the back of my throat where the whiskey stings me now, but clearly not enough.

On top of what I carry, there are the things I know. When something is seen, touched, or felt...you cannot unsee it, untouch it, or unfeel it. It's been that way since the beginning of humankind, that knowledge of good and evil. Once something is experienced, it's there forever, and has every intention of ruining you. My heart hurts for Eve.

I know what it sounds like to hear a man's deep voice turn to a faint gurgle, like a babbling brook getting smothered. I know what it looks like when a bullet sails smoothly, almost cleanly, into a man's chest cavity. At first glance, it's as though nothing has happened at all. The hole itself, so small and round, looks like it couldn't possibly harm an infant. However, when the blood, purple at first, begins rushing out, it's clear that the little Dutch boy's finger has moved from the dam.

That unique hue, the one that comes from the safe blue blood inside the body mixing with the afflicting oxygen upon its release, that's the one that stained me. It is a deeper tone than the mark I wear on my cheek and has spread over my whole body. However, I can't hide the vision of blood with my long hair, or with a distracting floral scarf. It's seeped all the way into my insides now, and it's never coming back out again. The whiskey itself doesn't have the power to poison it; it's moved in for good. I best ready it a bed and pray it will sleep sometime.

CHAPTER 5

SYDRA

"My father, Sid, he was a real charmer." I could hear my voice growing fond for him while I spoke. "He had sandy hair, grey eyes, and muscular shoulders. He was always clean cut and dressed like a gentlemen...as much as he could afford to anyway. He wasn't in suits every day, but wasn't in overalls either. He didn't make a whole lot of money, just worked in a factory like everybody else. Money was never a big deal in Tobaccoville, like it is in other towns, probably because there was no money in Tobaccoville. Everybody loved him because he was just so...*alluring*, I suppose is the right word.

After James Leonard Brawley left for good, Mama couldn't believe Sid chose her. Like I said before, she was definitely pretty, but, well, like a dandelion that had already been plucked. By the time she got with my Daddy she was just someone that used to be alive in some other time, you know?" I looked at Dr. Garris, making sure he was following me.

He nodded, as if to say, "Go on," and continued writing.

"My father was a little ahead of her in school, and

she'd admired him for as long as she could remember, since before she'd ever been with Jimmi-Lyn's Dad...she just never thought he'd give her the time of day. He was the kind of guy that went around with beauty queens, not farmhand preacher's daughters. When he did notice Mama, even though it was years past his prime, she was smitten from the start, and then, just like that, I came along, and we were a family."

"You'd previously mentioned you were born five months after your parents married." Dr. Garris flipped back the pages on his notepad. "Essentially, you were a love child. Is that correct?"

"Correct," I casually agreed with him, though I think his statement may have been meant to provoke me.

"And this was just public knowledge? How did that affect your mother? How was that received in your small town in the early twenties?" the doctor asked as if he had an answer in mind.

"Perfectly well," I replied ignoring his attempt at pointing out the scandal. "My father tended to get away with the things maybe other people couldn't. He was a leader. He was charismatic. When he did something out of the ordinary, people just accepted it."

"Out of the ordinary? How?"

"I don't have any specifics," I answered too quickly.

"Ok, just keep going." Dr. Garris readied his pen again.

"My father was *very* well-liked, and *I* was *his* name-sake. That's all that anyone cared about. People want-ed to know me because I was the old star quarterback's daughter. It didn't matter that we weren't rich because we were respected the way southerners in small towns earn it. We were attractive, outgoing, and athletic. I was Sydra Bumgarner, and I was born the homecoming queen. I was tobacco royalty because of my father. I *was* the prized crop. As ridiculous as that sounds, it felt good. It made things easier in some ways. Jimmi-Lyn was a Brawley, a nobody. But for me, I was a Bumgarner."

"I see. So, why did you change your last name if you were so proud of it? Why did you break one of the few ties you still had to your father almost immediately after you left home?" The shrink asked me this nonchalantly, but he hoped he'd get a tug on the line.

"Yeah, Sydra Bumgarner is still my legal name, but it wasn't so sexy in California. The name isn't sexy anywhere outside of Tobaccoville. It's awfully...*down— home*. Paramour means *for love,* but like a side-lover, or a weekend lover. And I'm that to every man in the country. I changed the spelling and made it more than my name. It became my persona." I couldn't help but sound conceited because truth be told, I was a little bit.

Even in the inmate garb, sitting in front of a doctor who specialized in crazy people, I was so very confident and so certain I owned the room. I didn't care that he was the professor and I was the prisoner. I owned Dr. Garris' cheap ink pen, the old wooden-planked floor, and even the man desperately trying to show me his authority in his own cool, calm, collected fashion he'd clearly adopted. He was terrified I owned it all, too, but I respected him holding his own. Most people, particularly men, couldn't do so much around me. The arresting officer asked me for an autograph after he booked me. Dr. Garris had a good deadpan. I could respect him somewhat for that, regardless of the other textbook regimens he practiced on me.

"Is that how you see yourself, Ms, Parramore? As a 'weekend lover'?" There was something disapproving in his voice.

"Yes, actually, it is. I'm the fantasy men don't get at home. I'm everything their boring wives in white stockings and sensible shoes aren't. I get to be the dream, while they get to pour his coffee and hand him his hat on his way out the door. I see it as a privilege," I said knowing there was no chance of him understanding what I meant.

"I see," Dr. Garris wrote something down as if he'd determined something about me from what I'd said, the second time this had happened now.

"Anyway," I continued knowing I needed to backtrack out of Hollywood, "the point is my father was very esteemed in our little corner of the world. He was no James Leonard Brawley, no military embarrassment, no town joke. It was good for me, but not so much for Jimmi-Lyn."

As I spoke, my mind was flooded with happy memories of my father, happy memories I hadn't even prepared myself for. When I readied stories for my evaluation, I'd pulled all kinds of files on him from my mind. Surprise images were starting to pop up now. I couldn't help but smile while thinking of him teaching all the neighbor kids how to hit a baseball on a Sunday after-noon. He'd show them how to point where the hit would land with their bats like Babe Ruth, making them all feel *that* special. My heart fluttered when I remembered him delivering hot chicken soup to sick church members. True, most of those memories were more like looking through a window at somebody than actually experiencing anything myself, but they were dear to me anyway. There'd been good in my father.

It didn't matter if his attention wasn't directed at me specifically. I saw how people admired him, and I liked the way it spilled onto me. I had everyone else's attention all the time because of him. His attractiveness was my attractiveness, and his popularity was my popularity. I liked the way everyone fussed over him, and the way people were intimidated by his very presence. I loved the way waitresses at diners would blush just because he ordered his eggs over-easy. Honestly, I liked just about everything about my father growing up. I wanted to be compared to him and known as his.

I wanted people to know that Jimmi-Lyn did not belong to Sid, but that I did. I had that over on her growing up, which I felt fine about since she had one particular thing I had wanted. I thought about our childhood friend, Vanse, for only a second, then shoved it away. It was never good for me when I thought of him. I switched gears immediately.

I reminded myself that I had to try not to gloat so much about the ease of my childhood while trying to paint my happy picture - that would probably be counter-productive. I had to be careful of what I said, and I feared I was beginning to show too much. I wanted the doctor to sympathize with Jimmi-Lyn only just enough. I couldn't incriminate myself in the process.

"Ms. Parramore—" Dr. Garris interrupted my thoughts.

"Sydra! Please, call me Sydra. I'm sick of the *Ms. Parramore* business*." I hissed at him, suddenly annoyed at the repetitive use of my stage name while being evaluated by a court shrink.

"Ok, Sydra," he said slowly and softly, "you speak well of your father."

"I do," I responded.

"At what point did you start to resent him?"

"Resentment...strange word. I don't know how to answer that, or if I ever did *resent* him. Resentment builds up. I don't think I built up any feelings about my father," I responded worrying my directness seemed too staged. I honestly wasn't sure what my feelings were towards my father at this point, but I just knew anything that seemed to have come about long-term couldn't look good for me. This is the part of our discussion where facts mattered less, and how I handled it mattered more.

Dr. Garris sighed. "Let me rephrase that. I'm going to be extremely direct with you," he paused. "Why did you shoot and kill your father, Sydra?"

I paused for a moment, and looked out the window at a bird hopping so cheerfully across a powerline before replying, "We'll get back to that."

"We still have time today, Sydra, if you'd like to go on," Dr. Garris pushed.

"Tomorrow then?" I replied casually.

CHAPTER 6

DR. GARRIS

"Peterrr...what are you doing?" The voice I recognized all too well taunted me the second I left Sydra Parramore.

I'd barely closed the door behind me, still fiddling with my files, and couldn't have taken more than three small steps. The wrinkled man of about 70, who wore his smugness more prominently than his outdated cream suit with cravat tie, eyed me with one bushy brow raised.

Dr. Rathburn, originally from somewhere outside Wilmington, had gone to college up north sometime in 1699. I think it was actually more like 1897, but still, an entirely different century. He adopted the arrogance and superiority of the northern educated but held on to his spoiled, old money, aristocratic pompousness the South gave him at birth. He also stood about 6 foot 5, which gave him a false sense of authority over all that he presumed himself to lord over. Add the entitlement that comes with age and tenure, and Chapel Hill's head of the Department of Criminal Psychology was revealed. In English, he's my boss. His ideas are stale, and his answer to everything is an armless jacket and electricity. He should have retired ten years ago, but I'm still waiting. A lot of people are still waiting.

"Dr. Rathburn, what brings you to Raleigh today, sir?" I faked the professional version of the good ol' boy routine, forcing my voice up an octave for his pleasure.

"Well, it's not every day one of our own gets to evaluate a hot shot Hollywood girl like that one in there. Quite a dish, isn't she?"

"She's a pretty girl, I suppose." I humored him, but didn't need him to see just how good looking I *knew* she was.

"Well, don't get any big ideas. A man can get himself in trouble with a weak-minded woman as darling as she is."

"I think I'm doing ok, sir." I propped my heavy briefcase on a nearby chair, anticipating, much to my own disappointment that he wasn't done.

"That's yet to be seen, I suppose. I came down here to observe you with her. What a subject you've got there, Ol' Garris." He slapped me on my back, which was now growing moist with the afternoon sun invading the stuffy hallway. "She could make for some interesting research, don't you think?"

"Maybe so," I hesitated, knowing where this was going, where it's always going with Rathburn. "I've barely seen the tip of the iceberg, though. I haven't been able to scrape below the surface with her just yet. She's pretty fragile at the moment, definitely not as tough as she seems. This will take a little time and patience on my part."

"No sane girl just up and whacks her old man, Peter, especially not one as sassy and cavalier as she is. But, since she's a real pretty girl, she may be one with a future still. She might be a great candidate." His nasally half-southern voice was like hearing metal grind against metal. If he lets that occasional whistle slip on from between his false teeth, I'll lose it.

"*For?*" I asked, dreading the answer, and still avoiding his pasty face.

"You know what for," Dr. Rathburn paused, flaring his wide nostrils a bit. "Given the nature of her crime, she could use a more aggressive therapy."

"I don't think we're at that stage. With all due respect sir, you've observed her for only a matter of minutes. *Severe* measures shouldn't be administered rashly."

"Look, Peter, I know you're not a huge fan of the Transorbital Lobotomy, but there have been some fantastic results with doctors who know what they're doing. Think about it, a Hollywood starlet as the face of this kind of criminal rehabilitation, and with our department behind it. This case that just fell into your lap could change the methods in which we deal with the criminally insane. They could actually be *rewired* with cutting-edge surgeries like this. Can you imagine the research, the articles, the speaking engagements? I could go out in a blaze of glory, while you come in on one as my apprentice. Don't you realize the success this could yield?" And there's the whistle, right when he said *success*.

"Dr. Rathburn, I say this with all the respect and admiration possible for your expertise...but, I don't think inserting an ice pick into someone's frontal lobe is necessarily the answer here. I'm just concerned about the patient right now, and she needs further evaluation before any decisions, especially of such gravity, are made. She hasn't yet shown me any behavior that warrants something as drastic and risky as a lobotomy."

"Your 'patient' is a cold-blooded killer, Peter. And you have your career to think about. You could end up on the front cover of *The American Journal of Psychology*. Who better than THE Sydra Parramore to get you there? Look at this gift you've been given, all wrapped up in shiny paper with a bow on top." He curled his thin lips upward into a sinful smile.

My God, everyone is going to want a piece of this girl. I stared at Dr. Rathburn's cold, nearly albino eyes, knowing I had to argue on Ms. Parramore's behalf to keep a needle out of her head. I'd seen no proof of the 'fantastic' results with lobotomies that Rathburn spoke about. I'd seen a lot more drooling, slurring, helplessness, and loss of bowel functions if anything. No matter what Sydra had done, I didn't see this *treatment* as her fate. The electric chair might be more humane than this.

"Peter, you will keep me in the loop on this." He put his age-spotted hand on my right shoulder, staring me down.

"Of course," I responded as directly as I could. "I think we'll find a lot of answers in looking at her group dynamics. I'm getting the sense that the people in her life, and her surroundings, have shaped who she is today. If we break that down, we may have some answers as well as good options for therapy. I think everything she's delving into about her family could prove to be incredibly relevant, actually." I attempted to offer him the chance to be on my page, knowing he didn't like this 'new thinking' as he's referred to it.

"Group dynamics, eh? You still got your mitts on those crap reports that Kurt Lewin's been cranking out?"

"There's a lot of merit to it, sir. If you'd read some of the findings—"

"Don't tell me what I need to read, Peter. You're making yourself come off as a wet-behind-the-ears amateur right now. I've been at this science since before you were born, and I know hogwash when I see it. Kurt Lewin. It's horsefeathers, Peter." He cut me off, his voice a bit more raspy with anger.

"I apologize, sir. I'm in no way trying to undermine your years of knowledge. I'm saying that this research has been able to predict behavior patterns, decision-making techniques, and social responses. If I look at her family, which she seems more than willing to discuss, I may be able to determine her motivation for committing the crime. At that time we can decide what to do. I don't know that she's insane, sir. She may be going straight to jail. There might not be a treatment to conduct, nor any institutions in her future. I simply don't know yet. I just want to make sure that I investigate her mental state to the best of my abilities before doing anything rash and eliminating our favorable options."

"There are always options, Peter. Wouldn't it be amazing if inmates started to become cured from the new kinds of lobotomies performed now? Wouldn't it be wonderful for the tax-payers if inmates didn't stay jailed, and became manageable? Dream a little bit with me, Peter." I couldn't stand his overuse of my first name.

"That would be something, sir." I attempted to end the conversation.

"When do you meet with the girl again?" Dr. Rathburn didn't bother using her name. To him, she was just *girl.*

"Umm...tomorrow morning, sir." I felt like lying but didn't for some reason probably related to my unexplained allegiance to the doctor.

"Alright, then. I'll be watching." Dr. Rathburn picked up the flat-topped hat that matched his antiquated suit and sat it on top of his thinning white hair.

"Tomorrow, then," I nodded, suddenly terrified for our famous young killer.

CHAPTER 7

JIMMI-LYN

When I left the bar, I found Vanse waiting on the front porch steps of what I guess was *my* house now. It's so strange to think about it that way. I wasn't even sure I wanted it, though it's where I'd always lived. So much had happened here, even before Sid Bumgarner died on the front porch. Did I even *want* this house?

The yellow caution tape had finally been removed, and for the first time in weeks, no cops were sniffing about the sparsely sod yard. It'd been nearly eight weeks since the day that changed everything, but it seemed like it had only been five minutes. It still lingered everywhere. Death.

The fading white paint on the tiny farmhouse, that was nothing more than a cottage, seemed more distressed than ever. It was like the bleak color strained to cling to the wooden slats, trying to hold on just a little longer. Sometime during the investigation, the last wooden shutter with chipped grey paint just gave up and fell off altogether. I looked to the far left and noticed the brown door of the crude outhouse hanging open with flies swarming all around it. I guess the police needed somewhere to go but didn't bother cleaning up. *Great.*

Vanse was sitting on the unpainted cement block steps, fiddling with a blade of grass, when I walked up. His eyes were far away and different than I'd seen them look in all our twenty some odd years as best friends. He was gazing out at the eerily still golden-brown field, which somehow seemed it had been touched by nothing that's happened here.

The field seemed to exist in a different, untouched world that almost brushes ours, but where bad things just didn't happen. The house was near paradise, but just outside of it. It was in the real world, part of my reality. It was quiet, empty, and even too lifeless for a spook to live in. There was no life left for a spirit to wish to cling to. It's bad when a place is too void to be haunted. However, it gave me hope for myself. I was constantly haunted - so I must not be as vacant as I think I am.

Only the fields seemed to stay alive in this place, resurrecting themselves year after year. The same was true right now. I almost envied them, the way they bounced back so naturally, no matter how many times they were hacked down without reverence by people with intentions driven by money and habits. Maybe that's what Vanse was doing now, just trying to bounce back.

The Piedmont of North Carolina isn't particularly beautiful. It's just an 'in between', a middle child amid the more glorious regions. The mountains have that smoky, majestic draw, and the coastal plains pride themselves in their sandy beaches and endless waves. The Piedmont is just tobacco, but the winds from the other regions reach it and give the amber crops reason to dance, and that is something to see.

They didn't dance today, though. Today they were alive but reverent. Today they took a moment of silence for me, for my family, and for everything they'd witnessed not just the last two months, but the last score of years. This afternoon the wind was still, and the budding leaves bowed their young heads. They let me darken my door again with dignity, and looked away, letting me have my moment.

There was still a hint of a bloodstain sitting on the left side of Vanse. I figured there'd always be a little bit nestled down in that dirty concrete. Eventually, it'll blend with the dirt and rust, and leave the porch looking like every other in Tobaccoville. It'll be a tiny fragment of unidentifiable dirtiness we may even carry in on our shoes.

That little speck of filthiness is a lot like the town it resides in; I suppose like a lot of little southern towns. They tend to stay patches of dirt or sand or a mixture of both forever, the ones that aren't fabulous. Turns out, they're not fabulous for a reason. They hold too much pain to attempt to be a Charleston or a Savannah. They don't bid to beckon society's best and brightest, and they don't try to extend invitations to the rich and famous, which is perhaps why my sister never fit in to begin with. These towns don't grow, and they don't blossom. They weren't stomping grounds for the Fitzgeralds, and they don't decorate their one-laned streets with antebellum mansions to show how far they've come since

The War Between the States. They grow tobacco instead of cotton, rice, or indigo. They keep rocks on the roads, and they blare church hymns instead of Frank Sinatra. They stay meager in a purposeful effort to remain hidden. They don't want to be seen, and they know they're terribly underdressed. I understood Tobaccoville. I was completely made up of its dust.

I made my way down the dirt path we fashioned into a makeshift sidewalk towards Vanse, hoping he wouldn't notice I was a little shaky. It turns out the Irish part of my heritage wasn't so strong, and I feared my wobbling legs were giving me away. I adjusted my white linen dress at the shoulders, and glanced at the skirt of it, making sure I hadn't spilled anything on myself. I toddled up the walk, fully aware that I was fidgeting.

"What are you doing here?" I smiled when I neared him, only barely misstepping in my cornflower blue flats.

"I didn't want you to be alone when you got home. Didn't figure you'd wanna be here by yourself right yet," Vanse spoke to me as I plopped down gracelessly next to him.

"I appreciate that a whole lot," I replied, wishing I thought to chew some gum. "I hadn't exactly been looking forward to this. I don't think it's how most new homeowners feel." I giggled trying to lighten the mood, which hung like a thickness all around.

"I don't imagine so. What you gonna do with the place?" His demeanor was solemn.

"I haven't decided," I answered. "I don't know that

I have a lot of choices. We have to get through the trial first. So, until then, I guess I'll live in it." I shrugged and searched him for an opinion about it.

"What are we gonna do, J.L.? How are we gonna fix this mess?" Vanse asked wearing stress on his tanned face better than anyone else could try to.

With everything going on, I still just couldn't stop looking at him. The stone-blue eyes, strong chest, and dirt rubbed hair...it had me. He was so good looking that he couldn't even wear anxiety correctly. His plaid shirt hung a lot differently than the burly old bartender's had. He wasn't refined by gentlemen's standards, but he was a gentleman to me. He was a lot of good, but he had Tobaccoville painted all over him and would never be able to wash it all off. There's something about the tobacco tar that just sticks, but maybe it's also why the two of us stuck. Maybe we were just always too covered by the same residue to let our friendship fade away. Whatever that "thing" is, even if it's just a way of life, it kept us close all these years.

"I don't know what to do. I don't know if it can be fixed, Vanse," I stared down at my surprisingly dainty hands.

My best friend let a deep sigh escape his stubbled mouth. His breath sang the same tunes it did when he first returned home from the war. Nobody, including me, knew he was back for months and months. I don't know where he went between there and here, but wherever it was, it was because he didn't want to be found. He just wanted to be lost. Something had happened to him over there that kept him scarce for a while. He never talked about it, but he wasn't able to hide it either. The air leaving his lungs told the story of his thoughts better than his words could. What had transpired over the last few weeks had taken a toll on him. He thought the Nazis or the Japanese would be the worst things he'd ever have to face, but he was wrong. Whatever the things were that he still wouldn't talk about, even to me, that left him with the faintest limp, were now shelved.

It took another tragedy to temper the sting of an older one. It's funny how that worked. New worries came in with new seasons to replace the old worries. Sometimes it seemed to take new pain to drive out the old pain. What a twisted remedy. It isn't much of one at all, and now I'm starting to see why a person would want to be lost.

The worst news about the latest woes was that they couldn't be left an ocean away. They were all around us, not just the reminiscences of a terrible time a million miles from here. A man had died on my front porch steps, and we'd all seen it. And no matter what terrible thing the man might have been, no one wants to see the life leaving someone else's eyes. It sticks like heavy humidity in late July. It sticks far worse, and far longer than even tobacco tar.

Vanse's mind was somewhere with that awful day, and I could tell it. He was still putting things together about all this, Sid showing up here, the past, the image of Sydra with the gun standing over a man he'd watched her worship as a child, a man he'd probably worshipped as a child at times himself. He wanted more answers, and I couldn't give them to him. Not yet, anyway.

"None of it makes any sense to me J.L.," he spoke out of nowhere, confirming I knew what he'd been thinking while he was silent. "I couldn't imagine what he could have done to her or you or whoever when I first walked up that afternoon. I just saw a man layin' there dead who'd taught me to throw a pigskin 'cause my own ol' man was too damn lazy to do it. I hadn't seen him in years. I knew he wasn't perfect to your Mama...but-"

"No, no he definitely wasn't," I agreed, cutting him off.

"But—but then, I started thinkin'. I went through every memory, tryin' to make this add up...and as far as Sydra goes, I still can't. When she wasn't runnin' around in our shadows, she was in your Daddy's. I don't know what happened between them that afternoon. I don't have a foggy clue, but you..."

"I what?"

"He did somethin'. He did somethin' to you...didn't he?" Though it was timid, Vanse blurted what he was thinking, a little uncharacteristically of himself.

I was caught off guard, and we stared at each other for a few seconds before I looked away.

"Who? Who did what?" I evaded his question, knowing full well what he was asking me.

"What do you mean? Who have we been talkin' about? Don't make me say it, J.L." Vanse got quiet and looked down at his mud-caked work boots.

I turned away from him and pursed my lips together. The time had come. Something that I thought people never knew, or if they did, had never asked me about, was about to be talked about on the open right here on this disgusting porch on a day that should have been pretty. I knew what he meant, the things he was pretty sure he knew now, the things he may have suspected in dark places all along. He suspected the things my own mother had to have at least entertained, but never had the guts to stand up against even for my sake. I suddenly felt my own nakedness in realizing, despite my best attempts, I hadn't hidden a thing.

I didn't want to have this conversation. Ever. I didn't want to look anymore damaged to him. I already wore what Sydra coined 'strawberry jelly' on half my face, which I know he felt sorry for me over. He already felt bad enough for the *almost* pretty girl. I didn't want to be branded with *this* too, even though I guess I already was. I didn't want to speak it into existence, even though I knew what had happened to me was obvious. Evidently, things like that brand even worse than birthmarks.

While I avoided his face, which I knew was sad in my honor, I saw my past everywhere around me. Everything about my entire life was spread like the young seeds in the field all over this place. The dirty windows to my back still radiated heat, searing into my skinny shoulder blades, from venomous eyes. I could feel the presence there, still waiting to catch me in a weak moment, catch me alone, *always* watching.

My secrets were naked now, and Vanse knew them all. He knew what had happened to me all those years ago. He knew why I always had bruises, why I tried to keep unassuming, why I always volunteered to leave the house for errands, and worst of all, why I'd never be able to bear my own children. He knew the filth, the sickness, the rawness of it all. He knew what I thought I had carried quietly, and he knew what I hoped would never have to touch anyone else. Now he was lifting up the edge of Pandora's Box. I wasn't even sure myself what all might come out of it. It had lay still and shut for a long time now.

I glanced back at Vanse, not able to help it, needing to see his reaction like needing to suck air into a rotted back tooth. His attractiveness still makes me feel sick and excited all at once. Even while the most awful of memories consume me, he makes my stomach jump. In a way, I longed for him to know every little thing about me, and in another way, I wanted him to know nothing. He had always been my rock and hard place. Probably always would be, too.

"J.L., you've been my best friend our entire lives. I knew things weren't perfect for you. I just didn't know how *imperfect* they were. I thought you just took licks for shit like the rest of us did. Everybody got the strap once in a while, and maybe a little too hard now and then. It was hard times, and high stress back then...everyone losin' what little they had. But it was more with you wasn't it?"

I said nothing back to him, just sat in silence, trying to threaten my eyes with the fury of hell if they let a tear escape without my permission.

"Looking back at it, the things that confused me as a kid make sense now...really awful sense. The answers turned out to be a helluva lot worse than the questions, and you've been carryin' it by yourself all this time. I'm sorry it took me so long to put it together. I don't know how it did, and I'm so sorry. I wish I coulda..." He didn't know how to finish his sentence. He knew there was no 'wish I coulda' in matters like this.

I could feel the pressure building behind my eyes when he spoke. It was pushing hard against me, and I could feel it winning. I hadn't cried over this in a long time. I had cried for others on rare occasions through the years, but I never cried for myself anymore. I'd quit feeling cheated out of my innocence, and quit feeling robbed of motherhood. Until now, I didn't know I had these kinds of tears left. I thought I cried them all out a long time ago. I guess I had some in there on reserve, just in case I needed them.

Vanse reached out and put his large dirt-stained hand around my plain light-brown hair, lowering my head to his chest. He smelled like the grass after it rains in the summer, and I inhaled it deeply. He was so comforting, yet in some ways, I felt unworthy of being held. He was such a comfortable discomfort for me.

"It was that first sunset we watched on the back of that old metal plow, the one that used to sit about a quarter mile out in the field," Vanse started. "Rusty piece of junk had probably been there 25 years or more....holes all in it. It was the kind that used horses to pull it. You remember?" He glanced down at me.

I nodded and sniffled as quietly as I could manage. "We were about...oh...8 years old, I guess. It was the day you never showed up to swim with me down at Ol' Man Wilson's creek. I'd started home and saw you comin' across the pasture with your little bony scratched up knees....hair cotton blonde back then," he smiled so fast I nearly missed it.

"I remember," I whispered, fiddling with the hem of my dress.

"I started to ask where you'd been. I was kind of pissed off. We lived for that swimmin' hole, ya know. It was damn near a hundred degrees outside that day, and I was sweatin' like hell, ragin' across the grass towards you. I was gonna lay into you good...then you just climbed up on that rock that sticks up out of the middle of the crops, and used it to hoist yourself up on the old tractor. You were so tiny. Your pointy little elbows could have cut glass."

I thought back to that day in late summer when he described it, and could almost smell the floral fragrance mixing with dying grass. I could hear the summertime birds singing, and see the late-season katydids starting to scramble around. It's a somber time of year, still beautiful and warm, but slipping away.

Vanse trudged on. "I climbed up beside ya' to figure out what was going on, and you grabbed my hand before I had a chance to say a word. Then you put your head on my shoulder just like this right here." He grazed the side of my face, the jelly side, with his slightly calloused fingertips.

I could feel my cheeks warming when he did this, wishing I was still young enough to pay the intensity no mind. I wished I could still strip to nothing and jump in that water hole beside him, and never think another thing about it.

He continued, "There was that—that..."

"You asked me about the stain on the bottom of my dress." I came to his rescue. "You kind of chuckled when you saw it. You thought I'd been in a fight, bloodied my dress up." I half-laughed in a manner that in no way fit the conversation; I was desperately trying to be ok.

"I'm so sorry, J.L. I'm so very sorry." I could hear his throat making a fist.

"I made you promise to watch the sunset on that rock right there with me every night that summer. By the next year we'd found other things to do...but that summer, we watched 'em all, didn't we?" I playfully nudged him with my knee.

"You just wanted to get away, didn't you?" He was fighting to speak.

"No," I paused. "The sunset just let me know I'd made it through another day...and if nothing else, that was beautiful every single time."

CHAPTER 8

SYDRA

$\mathcal{J}$ sat in the lusterless conference room waiting for Dr. Garris to return. It had been 24 hours since he asked me to tell him why I killed my father. He didn't want to end the session but knew he had no choice. I wasn't ready to talk about that part yet, and he didn't know he wasn't ready to hear about it. I hadn't yet paved enough of the highway we'd been travelling.

He probably hoped my conscience would itch a little bit overnight. I'm sure he anticipated the stress would eat away at me and I'd be ready for full disclosure today. Still, he didn't know he wasn't yet ready for that piece of the puzzle. If we didn't finish the edging, he'd be clueless as to where to put it, even if he held it in his hand. I'd get him there in due time.

He walked in more hurriedly this time than he had before, and smelled like coffee, though I didn't see any. He quickly sat his Samsonite briefcase down and took his meager chair that looked no more comfortable than my own. "Sydra, how are we this morning?" he asked with a planted jolliness.

"*We* are just fine," I mocked.

He blew right past it. "Sydra, let's just delve right in. I'd like to pick up where we left off yesterday, please."

"Dr. Garris," I began, "you asked me why I killed my father. I know you don't see it, but that's exactly what I'm telling you. I'm afraid the reason is a little long in the tooth."

"Sydra, the issue is that we don't have all the time in the world on our side. I have a set amount of time to make my suggestions, and the clock is ticking." He paused with a worry I didn't quite understand before adding, "Your clock is ticking. I'm not sure we've been getting anywhere, and I'm not sure you understand the gravity of this." Dr. Garris seemed preoccupied, though he attempted an understanding tone.

I wondered why the sudden urgency, which made me more inclined to stall. "I'm gonna need a moment for a smoke break," I demanded before seeing the expression on his face. "Please," I conceded.

"Sydra, we've just sat down."

"They won't let me smoke back in the cell here like they did in Winston-Salem. This is the only time I can do it. It calms me down, clears my mind." I was more telling than begging.

He reluctantly shook his head yes, managing to keep the eye roll he was brewing at bay. I pulled the cigarette out, once again, right there in the room. Dr. Garris didn't even consider the chance we'd step outside. He knew better by now. However, I did notice he quickly and somewhat frantically grabbed all his papers away from the desk when I lit up, including the file I'd already ground one out on.

I put the slender roll to my thick lips and leaned toward him. He'd confiscated my lighter, citing the fact that 'weapons' weren't allowed. It took him at least five cigarettes to realize I'd even had one. More than anything, I think he took it from me to assert some sort of authority that he could feel was awfully fragile in my presence. Good for him.

He warily moved my direction making the flame appear with the stroke of his thumb. I could clearly see he had never done manual labor. He had smooth, uncalloused fingers that let me know he'd been white collar since birth. His age meant he'd gone to college right in the middle of The Depression. His family must have been very rich, and untrustworthy of banks. They probably owned the land my family worked or other land that looked just like it. That's how it was in middle Carolina. The land was everything to everyone. People like my grandfather were the wet nurses. They fed, loved, and reared someone else's baby. Garris was not from a family of wet nurses.

He lit the cigarette, and I glanced up at him from underneath my endless eyelashes. For a split second, he looked into my eyes the way every man does. He caught himself quickly, though. He was too professional to let himself be shaken. Three more seconds and I would have had anything I wanted out of him. Instead, he snapped shut the Zippo hinged lighter with my initials etched into the silver. He then jammed it awkwardly, nervously, into the pocket of his pants that I imagined were a blend of wool and polyester. I bet he was prone to chafe. Maybe that's what the attitude was about.

"Let's be quick with it," he mumbled and stomped a bit on the way back to his desk.

Maybe he was shaken a bit after all. I coiled my lips into a devious smile and watched him walk away. Delicious.

I stood up and sauntered to the window, contemplating what to say next. I had to talk, or none of this would work. I was procrastinating, and I knew it. I also knew it wasn't completely for the doctor's benefit, but my own. Fear was never my style, and I knew I had to get it together fast while Garris was still somewhat on my side.

I sucked on the end of my favorite vice while I watched the mid-day sun beat down on the concrete parking lot. I searched myself for how to keep steering as long as I could keep the driver's seat. I looked out into the distance, through the cloud of smoke I'd created. I let my eyes gaze beyond the asphalt where the Leland Cypress trees decided to take over again. So *very* North Carolina. I still couldn't believe I was here.

If I hadn't come home two months ago, none of this would have happened...but then again, maybe it was meant to happen. Something got me to the right place at the right time. And, yes, I do think I believe it was the *right* place. I believe, for now at least, that there are no accidents. Isn't everything somehow meant to be? Even my own nature, which made all of this possible?

I'm aware that I'm selfish, and I choose to own it since I can't change it. I've decided to let it decorate me instead of degrade me. It's who I am, and I've come to live with it quite comfortably. I believe it is important to adore myself. My own flaws endear me. When I first made the choice to return to the state I swore I never would, it was because I saw a benefit. I can admit that much, but it led me to the soil I was somehow destined to stand on again.

I didn't come home two months ago to watch the undertakers put my frail mother in the ground. I cried 99 fake tears around the time of the funeral, usually whenever I ran into certain people that made me feel pressured to do so. I couldn't squeeze any out at the actual interment, but I think managing some here and there helped my image along the way. I had to save face for the sake of the line of work I'm in, but I didn't have any emotion left for my mother. I was empty of her. Even so, I hugged family members I was afraid would get my dress dirty, and threw away nine pity pies the neighbors had brought by that I knew would make me fat, mostly pecan or apple.

I attempted to feel legitimately sad in secret for experiment's sake, but I wasn't very good at it, so I gave up. I wasn't very good at loving my mother and was even worse at loving where I came from. I didn't have enough actress in me to fake it all the way, but I gave it a good shot. I was proud of that at least.

I hadn't been back home since I followed Dan McCreedy to California in 1939. I was two months shy of graduating high school but left anyway. I'd seen some things that hadn't suited me at home the week before I left that involved my father, something I'd eventually have to share with Dr. Garris. I let the pissed off kid win the battle with the adult I was trying to become, and threw my hands in the air. I ran away...rode off, literally into the sunset, with a simple man nearly twice my age I met at a gas station three days earlier.

Dan went out west with his guitar, and I went with my sex appeal. I imagine things turned out a lot better for me than they had him. We hadn't been in Los Angeles two weeks when I left him sleeping in a shitty room at a run-down motor court on the east side of town. I didn't even leave a note, though I considered putting something made-up inside his guitar case to spare his feelings. I'm still not sure why I couldn't quite bring myself to do it, why I couldn't just give him the common courtesy. Dan was nice to me, and at least got me to California. Deep down, I hoped he turned out alright. I hadn't seen his name in lights anywhere, but I haven't read it in the newspaper either. That was a good sign.

It wasn't personal with Dan. His leg of my journey was just over, and it wasn't my fault he chose to be another person's stepping-stone. If my past had taught me anything, it was that there was a lot of merit to 'survival of the fittest.' I made it the theme for my life. I'm as animal as any a man might find in the wild.

I used that instinct well, and only had to sleep my way through five or six more men before I found the next highest rung on the ladder. Then I simply, quite methodically, almost scientifically, replicated the process until I got to the top. It wasn't the best part of the journey, but it was necessary.

I started with a bartender who let me act in semi-lewd skits about Navy nurses at his nightclub. I'd do a show, entertain him briefly, then sleep on the pullout couch in his office. After him, it was an agent who stumbled in drunk one night but thought I had a spark. Then, eventually, it was the vice president of a studio who promised me I'd be in color like Judy Garland and Vivien Leigh in no time. No more hiding in the dark shadows of tobacco stalks. My rise to fame was easier than one might think; it was a simple strategy. It isn't a process made for everyone, though, and it's ruthless on a really good day. I wasn't the only pretty girl in my position, but my teeth were sharp.

Ol' Dan's teeth were round and new, as freshly cut as an infant's. California was probably not the best to him. It was amazing to watch what such a beautiful place could do to decent people. California is a graveyard without bodies; it just keeps the souls. Dan had far too basic a soul, and far too kind of a heart for California, and especially for me. California and I can't help it, though. Someone has to be the grim reaper, and it's not a job anyone applies for, just like the uniform is almost never an ugly black cloak. The grim reaper is almost always beautiful and more alluring than it is that.

I felt connected to my new home from the beginning, but I think I was truly a Californian the day I experienced my first Earthquake. I was in this tiny little boutique full of things I wanted, but couldn't yet afford. I was twirling my hips from side to side to feel the bounce of the red polka-dotted swing skirt I'd tried on. I closed my eyes and imagined myself being whisked around the dance floor, cutting a rug with the best in the biz, the other leading ladies fuming with jealousy. I saw myself dancing the jitterbug with Humphrey Bogart, his strapping arms around my small waist, while Lauren Bacall stood by eating her heart out. I could hear the horns playing their liveliest tunes and could smell the lobster canapés emitting their delicious, mouthwatering scents. I was so far away from the land of Sunday hymns and canned pudding bought on rations. I'd gone to my future and knew I never wanted to go back.

Out of nowhere, the ground started to tremble and shake. A huge shelf collapsed behind me, smashing to the ground in a thousand pieces. Two mannequins fell in opposite directions to my sides, and directly in front of me, a freestanding mirror shattered to shards. However, right where I stood, there was nothing but a square of untouched floor temporarily serving as my safe house. I was going to be just fine in California, and I knew it. I was immune to whatever the charming state had that seemed to bring down the faint of heart. I didn't have the antidote for North Carolina and never had, so I chose to remove it from my world. California had saved me, and North Carolina was out to ruin me – and everyone in it.

I only spoke to my mother once after I left home, and I was all Hollywood by then. I wasn't dreaming anymore. Lauren Bacall still had Humphrey Bogart, but I had the perfect clothes, perfect hair, and perfect wardrobe. I met other Humphreys, anyway. They were suddenly easy to come by. I'd already had bit parts in three films and posed for six calendar shoots. I'd gotten off bar cots and into director's beds. I'd made it.

I'd just bought myself the first car I ever owned the day before I got her call. One would think she'd be proud of my success, but she was the furthest from it. She called to tell me what a disappointment I'd become for her and how devastated she was by me. I remember her begging me to come back home, begging me to make something else of myself, begging me to be anything other than what I was.

She'd seen a poster in town. It was the first one that went national - the one where I wore black fishnet stockings underneath a golden high-waisted bikini. I stood facing backwards with my stiletto heels lengthening my just-shapely-enough legs. My hair was pulled half up and hung in unbrushed curls midway down my smooth back. I glanced back at the camera, and at 'any man, USA', beckoning him to me. I'd never felt so powerful and accomplished in all my life, but my Mama had never been so disgusted with me. She didn't see it as my big break, but instead, as her horrible embarrassment.

I'd been gone over two years already, and the war had just started up. I remember it was January because it was only weeks after Pearl Harbor was bombed. It seemed the whole nation was in a state of panic and in desperate need of something to hold onto. I'd done the photo-shoot probably a year before but they re-released the pictures to boost the morale of the boys fighting, and suddenly, I had a name.

The pin-up got to North Carolina, and everywhere else for that matter, awfully fast, and I got a phone call. I don't know how she found me, or who let her through. I was very surprised, though, to find that familiar disgustingly fragile southern voice on the other end of the line. I don't remember answering, or if there were pleasantries. I don't remember if I was even happy to hear from her at all. I just remember where the conversation went and how fast it got there.

"Please, Sydra," she'd begged, "please stop prostituting yourself."

"You're one to talk," I sneered back at her.

"I beg your pardon?"

"You didn't get Daddy standing up," I replied coldly.

"I'm not going to entertain this. Jimmi-Lyn needed a Daddy and I'm still married to the man," she defended herself. "You're shaking your behind for every Tom, Dick, and Harry in the nation."

"Try *the world*, Mama. This war is global, and my picture goes with it. And Tom, Dick, and Harry pay really well, by the way."

"But look at what you're selling, Sydra," she pleaded.

"I have my first movie deal, Mama. It's not as though I'm layin' on a dirty mattress hopin' the king of *Tobaccoville* is gonna wife me up. I make my own money. I take care of myself. Maybe you should consider being proud of me...and what's more...I know Daddy left you. You may still be *married* to him, but I heard Mama. You're alone."

"He'll be back. He always comes back," she whispered.

"Oh, I don't think so. Last time I spoke to Jimmi-Lyn, she said he'd been gone for over six months this time," I teased her with my most relaxed voice.

"I'm glad you're so thrilled, Sydra. What is it? You think you'll finally get Daddy all to yourself?" Now she mocked me. I gnashed my teeth, and her tone went softer again almost immediately. She knew she'd struck a chord with me, and was quick to reel it back in before I could fire back. "I'm sorry," Mama said in a new tone.

"Well, I'm not. I'm bigger than this now. Nothing you say matters." I could feel the smugness on my face while I spoke to her. "I'm a huge success, and you're so jealous you can't breathe!"

"I'm certainly not jealous. I'm worried and...and I'm sick, Sydra," she added quietly.

"No, you're green with envy because you've realized I became what you couldn't. I got out. Everyone knows my name, and you can't stand it."

"They don't know you. They know Sydra Parramore, whoever that is," Mama mumbled.

"I've always been her. You just didn't know it. All that matters is that I knew it. I'm doing for myself now."

"You're degradin' yourself, Sydra. That's what you're doin' and I'm ashamed of you. I get looks from everyone. I can't go to the grocery store without hearing the whispers. You're the nation's harlot!" I could hear her beginning to cry. "You didn't have to—"

"That's rich from you since you were such a saint. You know what? Go to hell." I hung up with the loudest phone slam I could manage, unknowingly speaking to my mother for the last time.

Jimmi-Lyn wrote me a few times when Mama got sicker. Turns out she had some sort of lung disease that didn't have a cure. She was certain to die and wanted to settle things with me, but I had nothing to say to her. It didn't matter that weeks quickly became years. Her being sick wasn't going to change what she'd said or how I felt. It wasn't going to change her ignorance or her pathetic attempt at raising Jimmi-Lyn and me. It wasn't going to change the obligations I had to my career. I did what I had to do. People have fallings out. I'd made a life for myself and I wasn't going to let her pull me back to Tobaccoville from her sickbed. You never look back at a town burning to the ground - it'll turn you to ashes with it.

I hardened my heart and went through with my movie deal. Then came many others. *Talk of the Town*, my first starring role, was wrapping up when I got the letter notifying me of her death. I was being fitted for the last dress I'd wear in the film while I read the letter to myself. I stood on a pedestal while the costume designer hemmed the bottom of the green satin gown. I read Jimmi-Lyn's letter stoically while trying to remember not to slouch and cause a crooked hemline. I was *not* going home for this. I scanned the letter, judging Jimmi-Lyn's child-like handwriting all the while.

I continued reading with my nostrils flared and lips

pursed tightly. Jimmi-Lyn went on and on about how she wished my mother and I had gotten the chance to make amends before she passed and how saddened her heart was over our feud. She went on to encourage me to come to the service, telling me she knew I must care somewhere deep down. Perhaps it would help heal to say goodbye to her. Then she scribbled some Bible verse from 2 Corinthians that I ignored.

I finally found her youthful signature and was about to crumple the letter and throw it down without reading the postscript, but something caught my eye. As I was wadding up the simple notebook paper the letter, "V" stood out to me, and I smoothed the letter out again. *Vanse is home.* It was written so small I'd almost missed it, but when I read it, the breath left my body. My stomach fell to my feet. I glanced at the portly brown-skinned woman now tightening my corset.

"Umm....Lilly," I called to her.

"It's Lyla," she responded in a muttled Spanish accent.

"Yes, yes, of course...I need just a minute, thank you."

She left me be, and I sat down slowly on the red velvet chair beside the pedestal. I read his name to myself over and over again, letting it linger on my tongue like black licorice. It's the walls in his war barracks I fear I never graced.

CHAPTER 9

JIMMI-LYN

Vanse and I sat in silence on the front porch for a long time after we talked about my childhood with Sid. Honesty has a way of thickening the silence up, making it stronger, touchable, animate somehow. We sat there at its mercy until the dusk gave itself to the darkness. I could see the moon casting such a dim light on the porch that it almost could have passed for serene. I could hear the night songs of frogs, crickets, and other creepy crawlies all around me, and could feel the moisture in the air swelling up to create the dew that wouldn't be fully ready till morning.

My head hadn't moved from Vanse's strong shoulder. I couldn't help but think about the last couple of months and how we all got here. The events didn't have to do with anything that had happened lately. With Sydra in California, and Sid God-knows-where, the recent years leading up to the chaos at hand had been quiet for me. All that happened, however, had everything to do with the years we all hoped to leave behind; the early years that we thought couldn't hurt us anymore for the simple fact that they were so far away. That's the funny thing about the past. It seems that it has long spiny fingers that can reach out and stroke you from anywhere, at anytime. I think that's what that feeling is when the hair on the back of my neck stands up on a warm day, or a cold chill comes across me from nowhere; it's the past reaching out, in that eerily ticklish way it does, to say an unwelcomed hello.

When Mama died, I half-hoped Sydra would come home, and half-hoped she wouldn't. I always loved and hated her so much, but most of the time I just loved her. There were times I actively tried not to, but I couldn't help it. She was prettier than me, spunkier than me, and just more everything than me. I knew that's how it would always be, too. However, as jealous as I was, I could only adore her to the ends of the Earth and back.

I would drag Sydra around everywhere with me when she was only an infant, pretending she was my baby. She was so happy, too, the way she would wake up smiling in her crib, just waiting for someone to come pick her up. Her little white blonde head would peer up over the alabaster railing, blue eyes twinkling at me, pudgy arms reaching. I was so little I could barely get her up over the edge, but she'd stretch out for me as hard as she could, and I would manage somehow. I liked the way she needed me to scoop her up. Nobody ever needed me for much of anything, and they still don't. She was so little, yet she was able to fill up some part of me that had been empty until she came along. And it always felt empty again with her gone, even as her attitude towards me changed. I missed her. I missed my sister.

As the years went by, she only grew more beautiful on the outside. She was so striking that people would whisper about it when she walked into a room. I would hear them saying to each other how 'the little one is such an angel,' and 'it's just too bad for that older one's poor face.' It took almost no time for people to dote over Sydra and just feel sorry for me. One came so naturally with the other.

Her vibrancy somehow worsened my plainness in everyone's eyes. I don't remember at what point I started to believe that as well, but now it's in me so deeply, it has become my religion. I believe my life is tempered by hers, and I kneel at her altar, begging her to let me go. However, like the moon binds the tide, some things cannot be separated. She'll probably be the rhythm of my pace forever.

Vanse was one of the few people who never seemed to compare me to her, probably because he was just a kid himself when my fate was decided. He didn't automatically envision our futures when he met us, pegging me as someone's housekeeper, and Sydra as someone's trophy wife. He just knew I was his best friend and Sydra was my annoying little sister that drove both us up the wall. She would follow us everywhere, teasing and poking fun at me. She almost always reserved her brattiness for one of two things: she was either vying for the attention of Vanse or her father.

I was sitting on this very porch, in this very spot, when the cab dropped her off the day before my mother's funeral. I was nervously waiting for her and had only gotten word a few hours before that she was coming. I was anxious anyway, trying to get everything ready for Mama. I don't think anyone is prepared to put a parent in the ground, much less it happening before their thirtieth birthday.

I sat for over an hour waiting for the dust to stir on the dirt road in the distance, chewing my nails to nubs in the meantime. It had been such a long time, Mama had just died, and though I didn't realize it then, I think I desperately needed to hold my little sister. Maybe she'd let me. She was the last family I had left, and I held onto the off chance she'd just embrace that. I knew she hated North Carolina, hated this town, and even hated our mother. But, maybe she didn't group me with all those things. Maybe I was separate, in my own little category. Maybe she still loved *me*.

I could feel my palms getting sweatier by the minute, and I tried to calm myself down. I wanted her to want to see me, and wanted her to be proud of me. For what? I don't know. I'd accomplished nothing except survival. Maybe that could be enough. Maybe she would be impressed that I was able to take care of Mama, what little crops we had left, and now the funeral on my own. Maybe she would see that.

"Get it together, Jim," I said out loud to myself and continued pacing. Why was I so worried with what Sydra would think about me?

I put my shaky hands to my head and massaged my temples, closing my eyes for a moment. I'd no more than taken one good deep breath when I heard the familiar sound of rocks bouncing off a fender. When I opened my eyes again, I saw what I'd been waiting for. The normally quiet road was stirred up in what looked like a desert dust storm, and I could see the old Model A taxi, that looked too shabby for Sydra, barreling down our long bumpy driveway. I held my breath when the vehicle came to a stop by the crooked rust-worn mailbox. She was here.

I could see her from the shoulders up through the cab window. Her hair was still perfectly blonde as ever, though I'm sure it wasn't natural. Not that it mattered. Her hair was flawlessly set, with each curl intricately placed in a work of art I don't think I'm capable of replicating. She sat in the grimy car; the best North Carolina had to offer her, just for a second, taking inventory of her surroundings. I'm sure it had to be strange to be not only back in Tobaccoville but back in front of this house for the first time in nearly eight years. She'd been nothing but a kid when she took off. However, I saw a woman, by every definition of the word, sitting in the back of that car.

I saw her narrow calves creep out first, then the rest of everything I always wished I could be. She wore a skin-tight, cream-colored pencil skirt with a matching button-down top, and cream shoes with a navy blue ankle strap. Her lips were as red as the bad part of my face, with the top one forming two perfect painted peaks. Her sunglasses were deep brown with gold earpieces and sat perfectly on her tiny turned-up nose. She hadn't aged at all and was truly more gorgeous than ever. In that moment, I was starstruck by my own sister.

She wiggled to me and sat her suitcase, by a designer I could not identify, next to me and took her sunglasses off her porcelain-doll face. Though I don't think she planned it, she then threw her arms around my scrawny neck and held me tightly. I was so shocked that it took a few seconds for me to hug her back.

"Oh, Jimmi-Lyn," she breathed.

"Sydra," I exhaled.

I'd done the best I could at looking good that day. I wore a cotton dress, light blue, A-line, and fitted at the waist with a thin belt. I have a small waist, one of my few attributes I'm ok with. The dress was only frayed a teeny bit at the bottom. I'd also gotten some make-up at the dime store and been able to cover up a little bit of the birthmark. My hair was pulled back off my face in a small bun held together by my mother's sterling-silver hairpin - the one with a real white pearl on the clasp. I looked at Sydra now and wondered why I'd even tried. She'd literally stepped off the page of a magazine.

Across her shoulder, while she still held me close to her, I could see the crabapple tree we'd climbed so many times as kids. I remembered sitting in the tree with her and Vanse early in the Fall one year. Vanse had a cheap pocketknife he carried around as his prized possession. He was always carving things and was quite the talented little woodworker. More often than not, his projects ended up becoming pieces of dollhouse furniture for Sydra or me. That day, however, we were using it to peel the apples that had just turned ripe enough to eat. He'd just finished one for me and dropped the peel on the branch below us where Sydra perched in pigtails. She reached down and grabbed it up.

"Vanse, Vanse, look! I'm Jimmi-Lyn," she giggled stretching the reddish peel over the side of her face.

"That's real funny, Sydra," he humored her while reaching down to move the skin off her face.

He gave her cheek a little pinch and Sydra looked over at me and stuck her tongue out when he looked away. I remember thinking how silly she looked with her tongue hung out with her missing two front teeth. I laughed and kept chomping on my apple. We must have been about eleven and seven then, though it doesn't seem all that long ago.

Looking past her now, with the aroma of her fancy hair products under my nose masking the scent of the apples, I see that same tree just starting to bloom. Sydra's grown and beautiful with two perfect front teeth now. However, I never outgrew my flaw. Too bad for me, we don't lose our skin like we do our teeth. I wondered if that's the first thing she noticed when she saw me now - the strawberry jelly.

I inhaled her scent one more time and loosened my grip on her. She gave me one last squeeze and let her arms fall at her curvy hips. Her eyes, rarely wide, beamed at me for a second before she gathered herself. She opened her mouth and looked like she was going to speak, but instead looked beyond me. She took a quick breath in and stopped dead in her tracks.

"Vanse." Her voice went starlet-style breathy.

"Well, hey there, sight for sore eyes. Where you hidin' those knobby knees and elbows I remember?" Vanse let the screen door shut behind him and jogged out to greet her, looking handsome in a plain white t-shirt and Levi's blue jeans.

"Ha! I left them somewhere in Texas on the way," she joked.

She hugged him gently but pressed against him in no attempt for a lady-like embrace. I clenched my jaw, hoping he hadn't noticed her efforts, though I know he did.

Vanse picked up her smooth leather suitcase and led us into our old house that was painfully pregnant with all of our secrets and memories. Sydra clenched her jaw. She paused so slightly at the door that only I noticed it. I think she had a sudden cold chill.

Many things evaded her because of her looks, but not the memories, not the rough ones. Her bad memories and mine should be the same, but they're not. Her's are different, if for no other reason than perspective is everything. I knew what she would be thinking when she crossed the dirty threshold and glanced towards the living room where the mauve claw-footed couch sat. I knew what was in her mind's eye, and it was from the week before she ran off with Dan McCreedy to become who she was now. It still lingered there, and she felt it for a brief moment when she looked at the outdated piece of furniture that now had holes in it. A quick flash crossed her face to let me know she'd gone back in time, but she shook it off quickly. I wasn't as good at such things.

I followed her into the house, though it'd been so long, she felt like a guest here. I felt guilty for not showing her in while having something delicious waiting for her to snack on. Of course, I'd planned nothing. The icebox might have had half a jar of sweet gherkins, or a cup of milk in there somewhere.

Mama had only been passed a few days. I'm surprised I was even able to get the letter off to Sydra in time. She'd changed her number so many times I had no other way to reach her and had just hoped I still had a good address. She said she switched everything around so often to avoid stalkers, but I had my own theories. I overnight mailed the letter, and once everything was said and done, was just thankful it reached her, and she showed up. I felt like I was juggling so much and dropping balls everywhere. I'm not made for the circus. I have very small hands.

I knew things wouldn't be up to the Sydra-standard, but she'd have to be ok with it since she didn't have any other choices. The only motel in town had worse than roaches, and Winston-Salem was too far away to drive back and forth. She'd just have to be fine with it the way it was; simple. Home.

"There any wine around here?" Sydra made her way straight to the kitchen, avoiding the living room all together.

Vanse reached over her body, stretching up to the top shelf. "Aged to perfection," he winked.

Sydra picked up the mason jar full of moonshine, not wine, that he'd sat down in front of her. She should have known. Even though we were in the heart of Carolina wine country, no such things existed in this house.

"Ahh, indeed. Only the best." Sydra smiled at the jar, surprisingly ready to embrace her southern roots. I knew this was for Vanse. Had I offered white lightning instead of wine there's no way she would have accepted it. But Vanse had a hold on her that nobody else did. She probably would have drunk bleach if he'd offered it to her with that boyish grin on his face.

I sat at the scuffed kitchen table in silence. I tended to retreat when Sydra got around Vanse, and the years hadn't changed that. I watched her looking beautiful while shooting illicit liquor out of a dirt-rimmed jar. I just wanted to look pretty in my freshly-pressed bargain bin dress. I felt damn near embarrassed of my effort now. What was I doing? I felt myself beginning to chew on the edge of my bottom lip.

I watched them converse and laugh, feeling further away by the second. It was as though I were holding a snow globe, watching the people dance inside of it in their magical world. So much was going on, laughter, flirting, life. I was just outside of it, rubbing my protruding collarbones red from the nerves, and if I'm being truthful, also the jealousy.

"I'm...I'm gonna turn in, y'all. You know, the service is at sunrise. Don't wanna be up too awful late." I hoped they'd follow suit.

"Yeah sure, J.L.," Vanse said eyeing Sydra."Sleep tight...uh...I think I got a little more daylight left in me if you don't mind me hangin' around here."

"Ok, then," I replied and turned down the hall feeling sick, and also, for some reason, small.

I overheard him say her name so excitedly. "Sydra, one more shot, and catch up a little? I'd love to hear all about the movie star life."

"Whatever you want," she replied giggling like a teenager.

I walked inside my drafty bedroom and looked in the smudged mirror over my dresser. I just shook my head at myself. I pulled the hairpin out and my mousy brown hair fell down like a corpse around my skinny, pale shoulders. I let my arms go limp and the silver accessory fell out of my hand, hitting the floor in perfect unison with Sydra's empty shot glass.

CHAPTER 10

DR. GARRIS

J stared at the back of Sydra Parramore's bleached head while she gazed out of the barred window of the conference room. She was no more than three feet away from me, but I found myself searching for this woman, desperate to know who she was. I felt like I was in the room with an apparition that could only communicate with me at its choosing. I needed to change that quickly.

I was told to be careful of Sydra Parramore well before I started to evaluate her. The arresting officers, as well as the district attorney, had warned me not to let my guard down for even a second. Now I know why they did, though none of us have been able to put it into exactly the right words. They kept telling me she just had a way about her, a quality. They couldn't pin down if it was charm, or brains, or sexuality. It was just *something* I should be careful of that she carries naturally. I didn't know what the exact trait was either, but they were right, it was *something*. It was a 'something' that intrigues and draws while pushing and intimidating. It could both validate and emasculate a man all at once. It could make a good therapist like myself obsessed with breaking her, especially now with Rathburn breathing down my neck. It wasn't only his ill intentions, though, it's her *uniqueness.*

I used to pride myself with separating my emotions from my work, but now I don't know. That conceit she wore on her face followed me everywhere, and I'm certainly not numb to it. It irked me to no end, yet I found myself rooting for her. I'm a Criminal Psychologist. I'm supposed to be on the side of justice. I'm supposed to figure out what makes killers like Sydra commit their crimes, then turn them over to one of two places: the penitentiary or the asylum. I know if Rathburn had his pick, it would be something more like a cage next to a row of unsuspecting guinea pigs. He just wants his name in the lights hers has been in. But, if she doesn't start to crack just a little, I can't help her escape any of it. Not the pen, not the ice pick. Nothing.

I got into this field with the naive notion that I could help people. Maybe I'm the crazy one. It seemed like everyone else in my field, especially Rathburn, was more interested in *containing* people. They didn't believe in progress or finding cures. They didn't believe in establishing the roots of behavior. They just saw damaged minds and used them to play God. Most psychologists and psychiatrists, including my colleagues and superiors, have turned into sadistic, self-righteous, assholes, and they wanted me to play ball on their team. It just wasn't in me, and I wished Sydra Parramore understood this. I couldn't give her too much kindness, though;

she'd walk all over it with those sharp high heels that I think were strapped to her feet at birth.

On paper, she didn't look so bad. I found myself skimming her files again while she remained in her stand-off with the trees outside the building. When I first found out I'd be evaluating a movie star, I didn't know what to expect. I'm an educated and well-traveled man. I'd spent quality time with the rich, but not the famous. I looked up everything I could find on her and nothing seemed terribly suspicious. She was the typical story of new money and new renown. A southern girl of simple means decided she wanted to be a star. We've all heard that story, and we have seen it replicated many times over the past few years with Hollywood exploding and televisions putting faces with voices. More times than not, these kinds of women are highly insecure and often impressionable. I'm not so sure Ms. Parramore didn't fit that mold. I thought she might fit it perfectly, but was more skilled at masking it than most. I didn't know if she was razor sharp as she appeared to be, but she had a definite way of making people think so much. I hadn't fully decided myself. After all, she was capable of murder.

There's more than just her air, especially when she starts to talk. It seems like she only told stories as they floated into her mind, like none of it had ever occurred to her before, as if she had no plan at all. She tried too hard to seem aloof, yet managed to appear genuine while she did it. How is it that she was so detached and engaged at once? I couldn't tell if it was a gift or a practice. She responded to me like I'm here taking notes to write a movie about her life. She knew we had a goal here, but was purposefully evasive. She used her chain smoking for pacing. (I quickly made a note of this when I thought about it.)

I believed what she was saying was mostly true, or at least based on truth, but was being dosed to me somehow. It was an exercise in control. She wanted to steer this ship, her number one goal. That quality may be specific for her efforts to move this case in her favor, or it may be how she is altogether. She openly fought me for conversational dominance. I'm unsure of her motive for doing this, though I'm certain she had one. Was she hoping for an insanity plea? Did she want to avoid life in prison? Was she hoping to atone for what she's done? *What does she want?*

As far as her motive for the actual *killing*, that I couldn't place yet. I couldn't tell if she was truly intrigued with her father, or, if this was an act to hide years of built-up aggression. Maybe that didn't matter at this point. Maybe I should talk about the things she's brought up; let her at least *feel* like she's in the driver's seat to crack her. Perhaps she needed to feel like whatever she chose to divulge is her own idea. After all, I wasn't here to analyze why she actually killed Sid Bumgarner. I was here to decide if she's sane and make suggestions to the court based on my findings. I had to quit thinking and try again with her.

"So, Ms.—Sydra," I spoke to the enigmatic woman's back while she continued to gaze as though she were posing for a pensive photo.

"Mmmhmmm," she replied, no words, all breath.

"You mentioned to me you'd seen something that upset you before you left town with your friend, um, Dan McCreedy." I referenced my own scribble. "You then went on to blame your mother for your not returning or communicating home. Which was it? Your mother or your father?" I asked her this question, feeling like she wanted me to ask it, like she'd baited it with the little clues she was leaving for me.

"What do you mean?" She sounded far away, still not facing me.

"I mean, did you leave for one reason and stay gone for another? Or did something upset you whenever you witnessed whatever it was you witnessed that kept you distant? Perhaps whatever you saw encouraged you to run, and you lashed out at your Mother as a response to it. Perhaps you were indeed angry with your father, but chose to let your mother pay penance because it was too painful for you. Maybe you have been sore at your father about something too hard for you to process, so you chose to act out on the simpler things you're sore at your mother over. After all, you've murdered your father, not your mother, Sydra." I served my words to her more undercooked this time, hoping to provoke her a bit.

She continued to breathe in and out, in an increasingly less content manner. I didn't think she'd respond to me because she wasn't wearing the right facial expression for it. She seemed more naturally aloof now and less regimented. Something in her demeanor started to change and I made note of it. Maybe I jogged some memories, or stirred more up than I initially thought. Something plagued her and it was no act.

"I saw my father." She said this in a voice I hadn't heard her use before, and after a lengthy silence.

I paused, waiting for her to finish her thought, before realizing she wasn't going to do so. More games, perhaps? "What did you see your father do, Sydra?"

She gathered herself again for only an instant. "It doesn't matter. What matters is I killed him...let's just talk about that, now."

"The past may mean everything here, Sydra. You've been adamant about that yourself. What did you see your father do all those years ago?" I prodded.

I watched her start fumbling her fingers around while she began to lose herself again. She patted at her pockets, and I could see she was out of cigarettes. She started chewing slightly on her bottom lip and took a deep breath. She was calculating again while she tried to remain looking casual. She stared out the window searching for a focal point, a tactic I just realized she used to avoid anxious behavior. She wasn't doing well at first, but I watched as she started to catch herself. I could tell she's done this before, reeled herself back in from edginess.

I, however, couldn't tell how aware she was of this behavior. She wanted to appear void of thought, wanted to seem far away. I believed when she got herself tangled up in that place, she simply adapted to it. She was very good at her own shiftiness, and I imagine an equally talented improv actress. She rolled with what she couldn't control until she could again. She reeled her nerves back in on her own. It's rather impressive in one respect, her ability to self-soothe. But now, I needed to press her, stir her again. Her method couldn't work every time, and she'd just proven she's movable. A win for me.

"Was it Jimmi-Lyn? You've gone into great detail about your sister, and how everything in her life has to do with yours. Was it Jimmi-Lyn you saw with your father, Sydra?" I asked ,hoping for a hot button.

"No...no it wasn't," she answered before leaving the window and returning to her chair with a casual smile on her face.

I'd missed my shot at shaking her. I had to get her back to that fragile state, because I knew now, for certain, that it hid under there somewhere. I felt that it waited for me right beneath whatever happened just before she left for California.

CHAPTER 11

VANSE

$\mathcal{I}$ knew I shouldn't have done it, but I couldn't help it. That's a sorry excuse for a man to make, because we all make our own choices, but this time it was the damn truth. I could not help it, and I hated that. My whole life, I considered myself to be a man of honor, somebody with integrity, with something to stand for. I was a military man for crying out loud. I should be stronger than this.

Sydra. She rolled into town and had me under some sort of a spell from the second she spoke. She scrambled my head up like hen fruit, and I just couldn't think. Hell, I couldn't even move unless it was towards her. I was paralyzed unless she willed my bum war-legs to walk. From the second she came shaking up the sidewalk it was like she spilled a love potion all over me, and I was somehow knee-scootin' drunk on her. I'd never felt so helpless and downright doll-dizzy in all my life.

The morning after Sydra came to town, they put Della Bumgarner in the ground. The rain cleared up, and I was standing there on the dewy grass between Sydra and

J.L., staring at my feet. *I should have worn better shoes*, I thought to myself. My work boots were about all I had, so I did what I could. They didn't look good paired with my funeral clothes, but I guess they were better than bare feet. I honed in on them, trying not to focus on the sisters, standing like dark towers on either side of me. I tried to count the specks of dirt hanging on to them, but that was no use either. It felt like counting sheep to try to fall asleep - it's a nice idea, but it doesn't really work. People spend all kinds of time trying to redirect their thoughts from whatever might have them by the balls at the time, but it's useless. The mind is the mind, and it did what it damn-well pleased. The mind and the feelings are separate; not only separate, they're sworn enemies. One won't take the high road for the sake of the other.

I could smell her perfume; Sydra's. It was hard to tell just what the fragrance was made up of, but I could pick up hints of flower, wood, and a soft spice that reminded me of being on some coast the Pacific splashed up on. I wasn't sure if it was still on me from the night before or if the scent was coming from her now. I'd tried to wash her off of me that morning, but I'm not sure I scrubbed hard enough. Who did I think I was? A man trying to wash *Sydra Parramore* off of himself. Every man in America would love to beat my ass right now if he knew. I shook my head at myself, the man who had Sydra Parramore and was so cavalier about it. No, not cavalier even, borderline disgusted with myself. And, maybe not so *borderline* either.

I only hoped J.L. couldn't smell her on me, not that it mattered. She knew good and well what I'd done. She hadn't given me the cold shoulder or made any nod to last night, but I could tell that she knew. It was never in her nature to say anything. It just wasn't Jimmi-Lyn to do such a thing. She wouldn't show her pain, wouldn't go after people who hurt her. Instead, she'd wear it, but like an undershirt beneath a sweater. It would always be there, a layer touching her skin that showed on accident from time to time. Only she can't ever take it off; it'll be stuck to her forever. She won't complain, though. She'd just go on wearing it. I knew she was doing it right then. But this time, I couldn't help her fix it because it was all my fault.

J.L. had been my best friend, and nothing more than that, for two decades. I don't know why it wrenched my insides so bad to think of her imagining me with Sydra. I had no romantic responsibility to her, but I felt terrible about it, sick even. I'd done something I shouldn't, and I knew J.L. was thinking about it, too. She probably wasn't so self-involved to reel it over and over at her mother's funeral like I was. She may be keeping it on a shelf somewhere for later, but I knew it was there. I knew she hated it, and I knew there's no one she'd want to see me with less - her bratty kid sister, and maybe even her biggest enemy in some ways.

Deep down, for the sake of our friendship, maybe I knew more than I would let myself admit. Maybe there's a lot more about J.L. and me to know all together. I certainly didn't have the brain space for all that this morning, too. I could barely keep from panicking from having to listen to the two of them breathe on either side of me. They were like two wildfires closing in, about to make one big explosion. I just needed to focus on the funeral, not the two of them. I needed to focus on showing a little respect for the life of the woman who made me peanut butter sandwiches every day of my childhood. I patted at my neck; it felt like it was swelling up somehow. I wondered if I looked all puffed out like an angry lizard. I shook my head, tried not to think, and attempted to hear the pastor's calming words.

In spite of me, in spite of my guilt, images of Sydra continued to flash through my mind like lightning. Nothing was working. Neither the preacher, nor my dirty boots, were doing a great job of distracting me. *Maybe I'll throw them out when I get home*, I thought to myself, as though firing my boots would help me somehow cleanse myself of this.

I started to get desperate and felt my chest tighten up to match my neck. I'd already sweated through my undershirt and collared shirt, which happened to be the only ones I owned. I knew my jacket was next and I'd give myself away. I tugged at my cheap black tie a little bit, loosening it enough so I could breathe a little better. I felt like I would smother soon.

Nothing helped me. I just kept seeing her, first as a little girl with freckles on her peach-fuzzed shins, then as a half-dressed starlet crawling towards me in the same kitchen where I ate those peanut butter sandwiches. *Why me?* I worked in a cigarette factory for God sakes. My name is spelled with an "s" instead of a "c" because my Mama just didn't know any better. I'd seen Sydra with men from movies and magazines. She could have anybody. *Why me?* Why a poor Carolina kid apparently named after Zebulon *Vanse*? I'm a washed up soldier with a limp who crawled back to making Camels for living.

I guess it *was* flattering, guilt or no guilt. I wasn't self-righteous enough to try to deny that. She made me feel like somebody for a minute, and I think her approval had that effect on a lot of people. She was just so damned snooty. And God, how we all wanted her. Even J.L. wanted Sydra's confirmation, wanted to feel Sydra's charm splash up on her, just one more quality she could hate about herself. And that's another thing; I hated the way Sydra made J.L. feel. I saw how she tried to embarrass her and overshadow her our whole lives, and now I've helped her do it. I was the thing she used to do it this time, and I had all but volunteered for the job.

J.L. deserved better than Sydra. She deserved the life Sydra lived, the life where nobody dealt with retribution for shit they didn't do. Yet, I became just like all the other men. I chose the glamorous sister, and I wanted her bad, more than I'd ever lusted after anybody. J.L. deserved better than me too.

When I saw Sydra coming towards me, up that disgusting drive-way, I would have laid down right there and let her walk over my bare back to keep her high-heel shoes clean. I was taken by her, completely. The pig-tail wearin' kid I ignored and poked fun at for her flat chest had me. The girl who sang 'Vanse and Jimmi-Lyn sittin' in a tree', sticking her devilish little tongue out at us, had me eating out of the palm of her hand. I didn't even know how she'd done it. Her showing up was all it took.

I could almost feel J.L. walking away, down the empty mildewed hallway the night before. She didn't want to share me with her sister. I might have been the only safe place she'd ever had - someone, if nothing else, not enamored with Sydra. She humbly let me go anyway; but what choice did I give her? What was she supposed to do? Cry? Throw a fit? I knew it would hurt her, and I disregarded her, giving in to myself. Now it makes my stomach turn upside down to think of J.L. lying down in her lonely bed while I twisted the knife in her gut.

It's not really Sydra's fault either, though, not completely anyway. She was a damn strong magnet, no doubt about it; but that night, I made myself one too, drawing her right back to me with all the force I had left in my body. I wanted to be more than an ex-soldier sent home with body parts no longer working good enough for Uncle Sam to want them anymore. An ex-soldier banished back to tobacco hell.

I wanted to make furniture after I finished the service...I was good at it, too. I used to dabble with it, but it didn't pay the bills, so my daddy got me on at the factory like everybody else's daddy did for them in the Carolina foothills. Maybe I just wanted to prove to myself I could still have her if I wanted her. I could get her just as easy as any of those Hollywood types. Maybe I was just proving to myself I could have *something* not every man could.

While my thoughts kept racing, I could hear the preacher babbling in the background, "...ashes to ashes, dust to dust."

J.L. whimpered slightly next to me. She loved her mother, despite her mother's willingness to overlook whatever went on in that house, to the full extent, I still didn't know myself. J.L. was still heart-broken and wanted the tiny woman in the box back, no matter what her imperfections were.

Sydra stood stone-cold next to me. There were no tears, no body language suggesting any upset at all. There was just a body in a tight black dress with a scarf snug around her painted-up face. There was a woman I'd let own me, and I couldn't stand it. I couldn't stand her pointy push-up bra or huge dark sunglasses. I couldn't stand the sticky red lipstick. I couldn't stand that *perfume* another minute.

As they lowered Della Bumgarner's pine box, that Sydra could have easily upgraded, I could only think of one thing. I felt like I was committing blasphemy thinking the thoughts I was while the few people present prayed respectfully around me like they should be. When I closed my eyes in an attempt to join the reverence, I just saw the Sydra montage again.

I saw her eyes looking into me when she'd thrown back the white lightning without even flinching the night before. And I mean she didn't budge an inch. She looked straight at me and wanted me to know it, too. J.L. had no more shut the door to the bedroom, not far enough away for comfort, when Sydra slammed the glass down and just stared at me, daring me to touch her. I found myself in a standoff with the wicked queen, and I lost, bad. After what seemed like an hour, but was probably more like ten seconds, she kind of raised one sharp eyebrow up, as if she were saying, 'Whatcha gonna do, big boy?' She threw down the gauntlet, and I had to respond.

I grabbed her hard by the arms, just above her elbows, sinking my fingers into her skin. I lifted her off the ground and sat her down hard on the linoleum countertop, knocking what was left of the liquor to the floor. Her head bounced off the top cabinet a little, rattling it the rest of the way loose from the bottom hinge. It fell and landed with a crash in the sink to her right side. I kissed her collarbone, dragging my teeth less than gently along her skin, and she returned the favor by biting my lip so hard with her perfect teeth that it's still sore and swollen up today.

She had some kind of want or aggression or both towards me, and I loved it. I pulled her blouse open, finding anything but a young, flat-chested girl. I didn't bother fumbling for the back clasp of her lacy bra, but instead pulled it down by the straps to her waist, stretching it out so badly I knew it wouldn't be wearable again. She jerked her skirt up to the top of her tight thighs and pulled her underwear to the side, not even attempting to remove them. I ripped my belt open and grabbed at my zipper like I'd never touched one before. I was hurried, terrified, and hungry for her.

"Do it," she breathed into my ear through gritted teeth. "Just do *it*."

I pushed into her, gave her exactly what she demanded of me. Her fingernails clawed at me, marking my back, then fumbled for something to grab on to. I felt her arm swipe an old teakettle to the floor, but because of our heavy breath, I barely heard the aluminum clank against the tile. The act was raw, built-up, and a little quicker than I'm proud of today. Truthfully, I'm not so proud of any damn part of it at all.

When it was over, she pulled me back by the hair of my head and looked at me hard, almost angrily, and moan-sighed at me, fashioning her lips into a delirious half-smile. I leaned toward her, maybe to kiss her, but she pushed me backward so fast that I'm not sure what I was doing. Then, she simply hopped off the counter, coaxed her tight skirt back down over her hips, and walked away barefoot, bra hanging at her waist and shirt still loosened. I stood there, breathless and sweating, my belt still dangling by my side, pants undone, watching her walk away. She didn't say a damned word. Not a single, damned word.

CHAPTER 12

SYDRA

The nights in jail were the worst part. Everything else, though routine and boring, at least busied me enough to keep my mind still. My chats with Dr. Garris, meal times, showers, meetings with lawyers - it's all tedious and annoying, but distracting enough to keep me from going mad.

After the lights have gone off, and I'm lying on my saltine cracker that's supposed to pass for a bed, I live in my mind's world. It's as though my brain awakens, takes my control away, and sieges my body once the moon makes an appearance. During the daylight hours, I'm my own, but at night, anything can happen. I'm at the mercy of some other being that just lives next door to me. Any thoughts that wish to visit just walk right in at their leisure. And they do so without so much as phoning first. They simply show up, empty handed, not even a cheap bottle of wine to break the ice. There are no peace offerings; they just invade me and make themselves at home.

Tonight it isn't the murder, which is what replays itself most of the time. Tonight it's something else, something that has perhaps bothered me more over the past couple months than the killing had. I kept seeing Vanse's face, eyes cast to the ground, at my mother's funeral. It wasn't the face of the confident boy I'd always known, but one full of shame, regret, and embarrassment...and it was because of me. He felt degraded and dirty by touching my body, because when he did, he could feel me to my core. He knew where I'd been, could sense the large number of users before him, and could feel my emptiness. It was an emptiness I hoped he could fill while I flaunted it in front of Jimmi-Lyn.

He hated the taste of whatever I'd baited him with and wanted to spit me out so he could eat a bar of soap. Still, all I wanted to do was to breathe him in, have him again, because even when I did, he wasn't really mine. He wasn't there. I'd just somehow used the magic born into me to dazzle him for long enough to take advantage. He might hate me, but I only wanted him. Always had. My mind took me even further back, before two months ago, closer to 4 years ago when the war was in full swing, and I thought I had gotten the chance to see him on my own turf. I hoped then to have my moment, the one where he'd finally see me as a woman. However, I'd come to learn that the magic I was hoping for was still years into my future.

When things started picking up for me in Tinseltown, I was asked to make an appearance at a military hospital just outside of Los Angeles. It must have been about 1943. A lot of singers and actors signed on to welcome some of the injured boys back home from fighting. We were told many in the platoon that we were visiting were shell-shocked and badly hurt. They'd been stationed on the Pacific front of the war and had suffered a surprise attack somewhere on the South China Sea. They were taken as prisoners of war by the Japanese for six months, where they were forced to watch fellow soldiers get beheaded and worked nearly to death in between executions. They got regular beatings and ate nothing but soured rice full of mealworms. It was described to us as some of the worst POW treatment imaginable. We were cautioned to speak quietly, and not to touch anyone.

I'd been asked to do these kinds of events more than once, but only finally agreed for one reason. It wasn't the severity of the situation. I was even more numb to such things in my younger years. To me, the soldiers were just people I didn't know in countries I'd never seen. They were just something talked about in between my favorite songs on the radio. All except one of them, anyway.

I signed on for the event because one of the names on the list of soldiers attending was Vanse. I thought I had gotten my chance for him to see me in the limelight. I would be his bright spot back on American soil, a real, successful, beautiful actress waiting for him. I'd nurse him back to health, help him lick his wounds, and make him forget the war. Maybe he'd just stay in California, trade in his fatigues for a shiny new tux, and become part of my world. It would be adorable at first, how he wouldn't see how to fit in, but then he would learn. He would stay and forget all about Tobaccoville, and all about whatever his troubles had been. I would be his safe place and sounding board.

I know now that Vanse has never said anything to anybody about his military tour. I also know Jimmi-Lyn would love to learn about what it was that he faced over there. I, however, do know at least something of what happened because of that report, and it was worse than she'll ever know. I still can't bring myself to tell her about it, and I know it's of ill intentions. I have a secret with Vanse that she doesn't have, and though it's ugly, it's mine. I know something about him that she doesn't, and I enjoy clinging to it. I only wished that I'd gotten my wish, that it had been him who confided in me about it. But instead, it was a fresh young man with high spirits named Lester.

When the day of the reception finally came, I got to the hospital right on time wearing a high-waisted polka dotted pencil skirt fitted tightly to my body. I had a navy blue, cap sleeve chiffon shirt on and my hair sat in tight platinum curls. I painted my lips and nails the same shade of bright red and made sure I looked like the Sydra Parramore the boys had been dreaming about from their hell.

They had all the veterans in a big gathering hall not too far from the triage wing of the hospital that smelled like urine and antiseptic at the same time. Jazz music, something that sounded a lot like Dizzy Gillespie, played softer than usual in the background to try to change the atmosphere, at least a little bit, from a sick room to a gala hall.

I immediately started going around, shaking hands, and signing autographs. I was waiting for my moment to 'casually' run into Vanse and could feel my heart beating faster by the minute. I'd practiced how I would smile from ear to ear and hug him gently, as to not hurt any of his wounds. My eyes darted about the room as I scribbled my name on picture after picture. I'd cheese for the camera next to men in casts and head wraps while my pupils bounced everywhere. I tried to take in each and every face I saw while the photographer's lights blinded me everywhere I looked.

"Hey Doll, you rationed?" I heard a slightly hoarse voice from somewhere behind me.

"Vanse!?" I spun around.

"No, he got discharged. I'm Lester." My eyes focused on the man sitting in the wheelchair, speaking to me from behind a neck brace.

"I'm sorry, you'll have to forgive me." I forced the words, feeling jipped. "You sounded like an old friend of mine from North Carolina."

"Yeah, you know Vanse?" the young man asked, straining uncomfortably.

"I did when we were kids," I smiled. " I thought he would be here today."

"He was here *until* today. They'll probably never get all the shrapnel out of his leg. They cleared him anyway, and he split town two shakes later. We kept telling him that Sydra Parramore was making an appearance but he high-tailed it out. Crazy sumabitch must have artillery shells stuck in his damn head to miss this."

My face fell to the floor. Had Vanse left to avoid seeing me?

Lester could sense I wondered this and responded, "Don't take it personally there, doll. Vanse was real messed up. He hasn't hardly talked since our rescue. He ain't really in his right mind. The rest of us couldn't wait to get a look at ya."

"Where'd he go?" I asked.

"Don't know. Sorry to disappoint."

"What happened to him over there?" I demanded with a little too much worry in my voice to maintain my mysterious nature.

Lester's face got very serious, and he lowered his eyes. "What didn't happen over there, you know? War is a bad thing that seems a long way off until you're the one in it. While we were fightin' it was just explosions and gunfire everywhere...normal enough. No way of tellin' how many men you're killin' and if you're next." He paused and considered ending it right there, but could see I wanted more. "In that prison camp they had us holed up in, we were always in the dark, never got to shower, and were only fed enough to stay kickin'. Then every day or two they'd draw a name, and if it was yours, you got the choppin' block. Vanse got drawn one day, but his buddy shoved him back and took his place, Vanse fightin' and screamin' the whole time. One of the other guards pistol-whipped him in the back of the head. When he came to, he knew his buddy was gone. He'd taken the sword for him, and Vanse couldn't stand it. After that, he wasn't really right. He didn't eat for days, wasted to less than the nothin' we already were. If we hadn't gotten rescued when we did, he would have been toast. So, like I said, give him a break. It ain't you, doll."

I held my breath for a minute and could feel my mouth hanging open. "I need to take a powder. Excuse me, please."

"I'll be here all night. Bring those long gams of yours back over here when you're done in the latrine," he called after me.

Feeling queasy, I charged to the restroom and stood over the sink, my hands on the porcelain with my eyes fixed on the drain. I probably stood there for 20 minutes before just deciding to leave altogether. I didn't know if I felt terrible for Vanse, or if I was scared he was really gone from my life for forever.

Now, from an arid prison cell, I couldn't help but think back to that night when I was with him before my mother's funeral. Even knowing what he'd seen and the hurt he had inside, I was still snaking him, just looking for the kill. I had to have the one man I hadn't yet. He wanted me, too. He needed to feel like a hero again, but I couldn't let him have it. I couldn't let him feel the human in me, couldn't find the courage to give him something warm. So instead, intrigued, I turned to ice and got what I wanted. And now that I'm here, reflecting from my disgusting pit that is probably a resort compared to his prison, I think back to my chance that I ruined because I was void. I know now, even if I ever get out, my chance is over. It's time to let Vanse go. He was never really mine, anyway.

CHAPTER 13

JIMMI-LYN

Vanse had been a wreck at the funeral, and it had nothing to do with my mother. I knew he cared about her; he'd spent enough time around her through the years. However, I knew he wasn't so attached to her that it would send him into this kind of tailspin - chewing his nails, avoiding people, and twitching like an idiot his first day in the straight jacket. He's good at heart, and I knew this bothered him. He wanted to be respectful of my mother, but it was something else plaguing him. I had too much on my own mind to deal with the reason why he was so upset at that moment.

Over the years I'd gotten good at blocking out the hard stuff when I needed to. I'd shut out a lot worse things than this in my life, though this stung in a different way. I knew I'd have to put it up for later because it was just too heavy to add to everything else. Vanse had been with my sister, and I'd have to find time somewhere in the future to wallow in it enough to get over it; just not this day. This day didn't belong to Vanse, or Sydra, or me. It belonged to Della, to my mother. She deserved at least one.

I stood for a while underneath the oak tree after the small handful of people who'd come to pay their respects had walked off, sniffling into their hankies. I let myself cry for my mother, let myself grieve this time. I grieved for the tiny skeletal body in the box. I grieved for the ugly bare box itself. I grieved for a woman who was abused and left by two men, and the woman too ignorant to stop what was happening to her daughter. I grieved for the woman who probably thought no one would care enough to cry. I took a moment of silence for the life I came to revere wasn't much of a life at all. I even grieved for my mother's mere existence as her proxy. She never loved herself enough to be sad over her condition, and I'd become accustomed to stepping in for her, whatever the role might be.

I wasn't bitter towards her, though I know there were times while she was alive that I was. Today, none of it mattered. I was just lonely for her now. I was lonely for all that she was, even the mistakes. I know there's something in my head Sid knocked loose to make me like this, but it was better than being mad. I figured being a doormat was better than being a monster. But also, she wasn't all bad. I also mourned the woman who cleaned my scrapes, kissed my bruises, and sang *I'll Fly Away* under her breath on Sundays. I missed the woman who was so beautiful the four times I heard her laugh. Truthfully, I just wanted my mother back, and I think that's natural. I felt like an orphan now, pushing 30 years old. I was truly alone, and I wanted the flawed, imperfect woman who carried me inside her own body back with me. However, the longer I stood there, the more aware I became that would never happen. The sadness was too much, and my eyes were too small to let it all out.

The third time they threw dirt on the box was the last time I could stand it. The sound was awful - the way the hard earth splattered out against the cheap wood. It was quick and reckless, void of any solemnness. It was a job for men in dirty pants who cursed too much. She wasn't there anyway. Her spirit was gone, and I knew I needed to walk away. I tossed a jonquil I'd picked on top of the last layer of dirt and walked off. I couldn't afford a nice arrangement, and I guess Sydra had other obligations. She was too busy to mess with such details. I tried not to be sick about that either and tried to remember how her life isn't simple like mine.

Vanse took off as soon as the preacher said, "Amen." I was ok with that. I knew why, and he'd face me when he could. I wasn't ready to make the small talk with him anyway. I didn't have the capacity for it just yet, and for maybe the first time, was glad he wasn't around.

Sydra lingered outside the fence, daintily propped up against it, one arm crossed, supporting the other elbow while she smoked casually. She didn't seem happy or sad, just there. I never did get a decent read on her that morning. She was mostly hidden underneath the airy scarf wrapped around her face. I don't think she wanted people to be able to read her on purpose.

She'd only been in town a day, and I was already tiring of her. I could have used a little time just to be by myself, but she wasn't due to leave until the morning. Maybe I'd just go to bed when we got back to the house and wake up in a new day with all this behind me. Any day has to be better than funeral day, right?

"You ready?" I asked Sydra quietly.

She didn't answer, just threw down the cigarette right outside the iron cemetery gate and ground it out with the ball of her slick black pump. She wore no feeling on what parts of her face I could see, and moved as though she'd over-starched her dress.

She got in the car with me, which I hoped she wouldn't have comments about. It was an old Ford in terrible shape that had been red at some point but was now more rust than anything. It looked kind of like the underside of a tomato that had been left lying on the ground too long. I wasn't sure she'd sit down in it, but it was her only way back. She'd ridden in with a taxi and had refused to come early with me to meet with the pastor about the eulogy. I guess she was too exhausted from her exciting evening the night before. I felt my mouth turn down and nose snarl for a brief second while I thought about it. I shook the expression off my face when I leaned over and opened the heavy door for her to get in. She only barely grimaced when sitting down in the front seat by me, at which I only barely rolled my eyes.

"I slept with Vanse last night." She took me by complete surprise when I

started the engine, though I didn't show it.

"I know," I replied dryly, hands at ten and two, eyes

straight ahead.

"Alright, then," she said back to me, cracking the window as though she were the one who needed fresh air.

We sat in silence for the remainder of the ride home, which was about 12 miles. It was a weighty silence, and I couldn't wait to be relieved of it. My throat was trying to make me cry, but I kept swallowing. I wasn't gonna let the poison in me come spewing out in front of my sister. I'd prevent it anyway I could, just like a dog chewing up mouthfuls of grass to keep his vomit down. I knew if I swallowed enough times it would hold back the dam. You can trick your body into not reacting the way it wants to. I learned that a long time ago. My mouth was completely dry by the time we got back, but, dammit, so were my cheeks.

I pulled into our dusty driveway, and the car threw up grime and rocks all over the place. I could hear the pebbles bouncing off the metal underside of the car. The huge potholes in the road made it impossible to get in cleanly, but I was used to it. Sydra coughed at the dirt swirling around us and dramatically waved her gloved hand back and forth to shoo it away.

"Really, that's what makes you cough," I giggled a little, smiling for the first time that day. "You smoke like a freight train runnin' hot."

"Different kinda smoke," she replied lightly, almost cracking a smile herself.

I shook my head at her, amused, when she looked past me, her eyes growing wider by the second. I didn't know what she saw, but I knew it couldn't be Vanse, she looked too awe-stricken - even for him. It had to be something else. I half expected to find the house on fire. I narrowed my eyes, confused for a minute, then saw a figure in a short-sleeved button-down shirt sitting on the porch beyond us. The dust was too thick and at first I couldn't see who it was.

Sydra got out of the car quickly and jogged up the driveway, stopping at the bottom of the three concrete steps leading into the house. I grabbed my bag, opened my creaky door and trailed behind her, assuming another neighbor had stopped by with a casserole I'd be happy to drown my sorrows with. Maybe it was another old flame or someone she hadn't seen in a while.

Then I heard her speak. "Daddy?" she whispered, and then squealed like a little girl on Christmas morning.

I stopped dead in my tracks about five feet from the edge of the porch. I had just dropped my keys into my handbag and slowly looked up. I now had a perfect view of Sid Bumgarner standing up off my front porch swing walking towards Sydra. He was getting chrome-domed on top, and his sideburns were now accented with grey wires. A potbelly resided in his middle where a strong athletes stomach used to live and his face had a few more lines than I remembered. I looked hard at the man, hoping my eyes were deceiving me, but it was definitely Sid, right in front of me, in the flesh.

"Long time, no see, Princess!" Sid replied to his daughter sweetly, but to me, his voice was like dragging a bent-pronged fork over clean China.

"I can't believe you're here, Daddy!" Sydra threw her arms around his thick leathery neck.

"Thought I'd come pay some respect. I've been back a few weeks...been staying over in Winston. I saw the obituary in the paper. Damn shame, ain't it?" He faked sympathy in his gruff voice, shaking his head like he had a soul.

"Oh, Daddy! I'm just so glad you came!" She was still shrieking with excitement.

I continued to stand dazed at the edge of the driveway. I tried to find my voice, but my throat initiated an emergency lockdown. I tried to scrape together the words to demand that he get off *my* property right now, but I couldn't.

"Jimmi-Lyn," Sid nodded to me when Sydra reluctantly released him.

When he said my name I felt my entire body go cold, and my fingertips tingle with panic. I let my purse leave my hand when my knees gave, and I was on the ground.

CHAPTER 14

SYDRA

$\mathcal{D}$r. Garris kept pressing me, and he was asking all the questions I needed him to ask. I'd drop clues for him like breadcrumbs, and he'd eat them up. Piece by piece, he ambled down my trail.

He asked me about the reason I left Tobaccoville to begin with, which I'd needed him to do, picking up his breadcrumb like a good boy. However, my mind seemed like it wanted to work on its own freewill there for a minute. I didn't need unplanned memories popping up to cloud my judgement. But, I think I've got a hold on it now, and I won't let it go again.

I would continue to let the good doctor drag the information out of me, bit by bit. In return, I would give him my perfectly planned answers, no room for errors. He could coax what he needed out of me like a needle pulling thread, as long as he never realized he would sew my masterpiece from pre-drawn plans. It would be perfect.

"Sydra, this entire time, you have spoken a great deal about a small handful of people in your life: Jimmi-Lyn, James Leonard Brawley, your father, your mother, and Vanse. Most of all, though, it's been your relationship with your sister and your father that you've honed in on. You went so far as to tell me that Jimmi-Lyn's past has everything to do with this. Now, you're telling me that whatever you saw that was so upsetting about your father...upsetting enough to make you leave town with a drifter, in fact, DID NOT, have anything to do with Jimmi-Lyn. Is that correct?" Dr. Garris was half asking me the question and half recapping for himself.

"No, it did not," I replied emphatically. "But the situation does have to do with her. I'm getting to that. *Patience, Doctor.*"

"Let's stick to the topic for a moment, Sydra." He ignored my provocation. "Is whatever you saw involving your father the reason you stayed gone from home all this time?"

A direct question - hard to avoid.

"Yes and no," I replied, seated once again. "I was angry at my father when I left, but I wouldn't say I held any grudges towards him that kept me away. Those were more directed at my mother. My mother wasn't my father's scapegoat. I just didn't want to see her after our argument."

"Then why bring up this event with your father that clearly prompted you to flee your hometown? If it was no big deal, why didn't you just go back home when you cooled off?"

"I enjoyed being away from my mother, and I enjoyed the prospect of fame. When you go to California, you don't come back. It's not that difficult to see why," I answered sincerely.

"Fair enough," Dr. Garris nodded, "but you did bring the event with your father up. Why do that if it's so insignificant?"

"Because it is significant, it just isn't why I killed him. I remembered it later and thought maybe it mattered. I thought that maybe it spoke to the fact that he hadn't always been perfect."

"Then, by all means, tell me about it, Sydra." Dr. Garris swallowed and sat his pen down slightly less than a cool and collected therapist, as himself, should.

I was getting to him. I could feel it. I no longer had to volunteer information to incriminate my father. My therapist had begged for it. It wouldn't come off as a grudge I'm unearthing, but instead, an effort to comply with questioning. Dr. Garris is doing a great job performing my dirty work.

"Sydra, just explain to me what you saw before you left home in 1939." His hands became a sharper version of an orchestra conductor's.

I took a breath. It was time to reveal a little bit of history; enough to show my father was no angel, though all I had ever done was adore him. It was time for Dr. Garris to start making sense of the information he'd been given. Soon enough he'd take that fancy pen of his and connect all the little dots I'd carefully numbered for him, then he'd sit back and admire a picture he thought he drew all on his own.

Nothing about murder is attractive. At some point, I

knew I would need to expose its gross underbelly. I just had to be sure it wasn't my dark side, but Sid's that I unveiled. I really did hate revealing the more undesirable things about my father because everything in my bones wanted to defend him, protect him even. He had a hold on me in that way, and I knew it. However, if I went with the natural feeling to build him up, where would that leave me? I'd done just enough of that already. I had to expose him as someone who had it coming, as much as I hated that. He was dead now, and I had myself to save. It was time to clue Dr. Garris in on what had disturbed me before I left for California....the Maggie Morgan story.

The best part about the Maggie story is that it was incredibly true, and indeed, the reason I first found the nerve to leave Tobaccoville. I wouldn't have to fake it being a sore spot for me because it was. What it would also do is show my witty evaluator how my father had done something objectionable years ago, affecting my response to him now. It would give Dr. Garris an actual previous event to link to the current one I'd yet to reveal. The one that led to my father's demise...the one that did involve the pitiful Jimmi-Lyn.

The best part would be when Dr. Garris feels like he uncovered all of this tasty information himself by choosing where to dig. He'd forget he's following the map I so discretely provided. When he revealed patterns of bad behaviors from Sid, Dr. Garris would form his professional predispositions about him. My insanity, when pulling the trigger, would prove temporary but his distasteful behavior will prove to be long in the making. I had to disclose it just right, though, in the proper dosage, just like I had when I'd spoken so well of my father. It could not appear as fuel for a vendetta against him. I had to be cautious when painting the picture of Sid's ugly side, being careful to not provide a long-time, revenge-driven motive for myself along with it. This nail is for Sid's coffin, not mine.

"I saw my father...um...*with* Maggie," I began gingerly, allowing just enough emotion to enter my voice.

"And who is Maggie?" Dr. Garris asked with an exasperated and somewhat flat tone, thinking I was sending him on a wild goose chase by introducing her.

"Maggie Morgan was my best friend in high school. We twirled batons together, lusted after Vanse together, picked on Jimmi-Lyn together, did everything together... she was always over at our house, like a second sister to me. Her mama dated my father in high school, which in a small town wasn't all that weird. My Daddy was still good looking as could be at forty years old. They had kind of a *flirtation*, you know? I thought it was mostly innocent...just him pickin' at her a little bit, and her gettin' the giggles when he'd walk by...strokin' one another's egos. Turns out it was actually a little more than that." I purposefully let my voice ebb into quietness.

"How so?" Dr. Garris asked skeptically. "I need you to be specific, please."

"Well, Maggie was staying over with me one evening. It was springtime, and I remember we'd been out running around with some boys earlier in the day. We'd gotten the town wino to buy some cheap beer for us at the corner store, and we drank it behind the barn in the field. We were all pretty lit by sundown and stumbled our way back to our house to pass out," I paused for effect. "When I went to sleep, we were both in my bed, Maggie and me. But when I woke up in the middle of the night, hungover as all get out and thirsty as a desert camel, I noticed Maggie wasn't in the bed with me. I didn't think too much of it. I figured she'd sobered up and headed home, so I started to the kitchen for some water. Our house was tiny, and the small hallway that led to the front door split the kitchen and living room. When I opened the refrigerator door, the light revealed two figures on the couch across from me...it was Daddy and Maggie..." I planned the break once again and let my eyes fill up with tears this time.

"And you walked in on this person engaged romantically with your father? Is that what I'm gathering?" Dr. Garris came to my rescue.

"Yes." I let a drop roll down my cheek, all in perfect timing. "My Daddy and my best friend."

"Consensual?"

"Yes. I mean, she was only 16 years old, but yes, as far as I know." I cried only slightly.

"What about your mother? Did she know about it?"

"I have no clue, but probably." I dabbed at my eyes with a tissue the doctor passed to me.

"And Jimmi-Lyn?" he asked.

"Umm—I'm not sure if she knew or not," I answered

while wondering why Jimmi-Lyn would have cared who my father was sleeping with and why Dr. Garris would have asked. I hadn't yet told him what I'd planned on connecting to Jimmi-Lyn with this situation. Was he ahead of me?

While I was answering him, telling him about my father and Maggie as I rehearsed, I started to feel strange again, like I had yesterday before getting myself under control. Thoughts started entering my mind that I hadn't prompted. I could hear myself talking without knowing what I was saying. The memories of the two of them together ran rampantly through my mind. They were troubling, and always had been, just more troubling to me at this moment than I'd anticipated. It was true that this was the reason I'd left home. I'd thought of it many times and assumed I would be able to use it to my advantage here. But new memories were starting to come with it this time, little forgotten images popping up in my mind's eye, disrupting me.

When Dr. Garris mentioned Jimmi-Lyn, that's what blindsided me a little bit. I never remembered her as part of this story, yet inside I'm feeling like she may have been there. I needed to deal with that later. I told myself to stick to the plan. I couldn't be shaken now. I was at the most critical point.

"So, you were angry that your father had betrayed you, your mother, and sister. Is that correct?" He went on questioning me.

"I don't know..." I responded sincerely, knowing I meant to give him something else.

"Sydra, in your own words, why did this make you so upset?" He spoke like each word was a separate sentence.

"I...I—I'd like to take a break for just a minute, please." My mind was getting cloudy, and I needed to go over some things with myself before I said something I may not mean to.

"Sydra, we need to keep going. We're making progress, here." Dr. Garris kept his voice very soft and even, worried a change in key would spook me.

"I need a break," I said again, wiping my dampening palms on my pants.

My lines were escaping, and I was terribly out of character. I was going to blow the whole thing if I didn't get a handle on myself immediately. Memories were flooding in through what felt like a broken dam that up until this point I'd been able to depend on completely. My plans were going to crumble because I was about to have an emotional response. I couldn't do that; that ruins it.

I needed Jimmi-Lyn. I needed to go over this again. I needed to ask her some things about that day. Things that made no sense were taking over my mind, confusing me terribly. There were so many flashes that seemed both familiar and foreign invading me now. I kept seeing my sister's face as Maggie's faded.

"Sydra, talk to me," Dr. Garris pressed. "It's all right there. Tell me what you want to tell me, Sydra. I can tell you're here with me. I can help you through this. Go ahead and let out whatever it is you're trying to fight."

"I want a break." I refused to respond with any other statement.

"Why did you kill your father, Sydra?" Dr. Garris dared to touch what he saw as the hottest of all the buttons.

"I killed my father!" I insisted for no reason, immediately wondering why I'd said that.

"I know that, Sydra. Why? Why did you pull the trigger that day?" he urged.

"I want a break." I went to my safe zone again.

"Sydra, just stay calm." Dr. Garris was now on his feet; hands stretched out like he was facing an armed enemy.

Did I frighten him? How erratically was I acting? I had to get out of the room that I felt was getting tinier by the second. Images of my father, of Maggie, of Jimmi-Lyn, seemed to swirl around me like a tornado.

I ran to the door of the office and began beating on it with all my might, crying and screaming frantically. "Let me out of here, now! I want out! Guard, GUARD!" My stomach dropped, lurched, and heaved. My poker face was gone.

CHAPTER 15

DR. GARRIS

$\mathcal{T}$he doors to the conference room burst open, and two guards rushed in to manhandle Sydra away. At that moment, the intriguing actress that I had to force myself not to stare at left, and a disturbed inmate slinging snot and tears filled the uniform that suddenly looked at home around her body. Something had changed, and it wasn't just the mood. Sydra was gone. Someone else entirely had set up shop, and now used her bones to thrash about in the officer's meat hooks.

"That's enough for now," the older of the two scoffed, feeling special about his authority. "I'll get someone in here to clean this mess up. Good going, makin' her sick, Doc." He wrinkled his porkish nose up and guided her out the door around her vomit.

I balled my fist up and brought it down hard on top of the wobbling table. Dr. Rathburn shuffled in, this time with his ivory-handled cane in tow that I'd come to think was just for looks. He passed by Sydra, seemingly pleased to witness her in the throes of hysterics.

"Great job with your new methods, Peter! Clearly, you've made a breakthrough exploring these...what is it? Group dynamics?"

I looked him in the eye for a second, long enough to decide I had nothing to say.

"Are you ready to end your fact-finding mission, and declare that girl insane yet?" His voice was weak but vehement.

"She got upset because I was getting to her. It isn't always calm and pretty. We *did* almost have a breakthrough!" I tried to keep my voice even but struggled with it.

"You can't get anywhere with lunatics, Peter! I'm trying to tell you. It can't be done. She needs to be deemed incompetent, and then I can pull the strings needed to get her turned over to the University. We can help her there and report on the progress. Then, maybe, we can avoid outbursts like this with other criminals."

"People have outbursts, Rathburn. It's called emotions. It doesn't mean they're crazy or can't be helped — quite the contrary. The repression is what causes the hysterics."

"Peter, I remember you as a student of mine. You were one of the very brightest, graduated at the top of your class. I knew you would be my successor one day. But now...now, you spout off like some sort of quack. You need to come back to the home team before you ruin yourself." He waited for the response I didn't offer. "Fill out your little forms, and I'll have her turned over to us. Exploring your other avenues has been, *admirable,* in a respect. It's good science to ask the occasional question but you know it's time to let that go. Trust that I know better than you this time." He took on an almost fatherly tone now, a new tactic. How tired I was getting of people trying to *handle* me.

"She hasn't even been tried yet. It isn't our right to make that call for her. Also, that outburst was anxiety based. I don't think she's crazy and I'm not going to declare a person insane if my medical evaluation tells me she isn't. I think she may be on the brink of discovering some repressed memories. I think I can help her do that."

"Repressed memories, my ass! You think you're Sigmund Freud now? Jesus, Peter!"

"You need to let me do my job!" I fired back.

"What I'm about to do is have you taken off this case, and reviewed by the department!"

"For what? Refusing to lobotomize an undiagnosed, untried suspect in a murder case?"

"For not listening," he hissed and slammed his cane towards the ground.

"Fine. Do it. Go file your paperwork, and try to find someone else to cover this. You know you aren't well enough to do it yourself. I'll have this case closed before you get that far, and I will have you under review for attempting to skirt our legal system in your fame-hungry attempt at last minute recognition. You are exploiting this woman, and I won't stand for it!" I shouted.

"You'll be sorry, Peter."

"No, you will be, *Myron*." I taunted him with the use of his first name.

I rushed passed him, my briefcase nudging him

enough to make a statement. I could feel my jaw clenched tightly and I made my way down the elevator and out to the parking lot. I wondered if Sydra knew what fate she might come to. I had to get to her fast. Time had never been more of the essence for her. This case needed answers and she'd better start talking before someone over my head takes that chance away from her forever.

CHAPTER 16

JIMMI-LYN

ℐ couldn't stop thinking about how Sydra's evaluation was going. The worry followed me everywhere. I could feel it lingering about shoulder high, breathing down the back of my neck with its hot breath everywhere I went. Whenever I tried to shoo it away, it just laughed at me and breathed harder until I found myself completely emerged in its steam.

I didn't want my sister to go to jail or the nut house. I knew she had a plan and she was sure it would work. But, I had no way of knowing how it was all going, and it was driving me crazy. The worst part was that I knew this was all my fault. If it weren't for me, she wouldn't be sitting in a jail cell right now. No, she would be back in Hollywood, probably on a glamorous set, surrounded by beautiful people. Her biggest worry would be trying to memorize her next lines. Instead, a day and a half in my world put her behind bars. If this doesn't work, and she gets convicted, I don't think I can live with myself.

"Where's that mind of yours, J.L.?" Vanse walked in

and sat a glass of sweet tea down in front of me.

He constantly worried about me, which kept him at my house. I didn't want him to go out his way for me, or feel obligated to stay, but I'd be lying if I said I hadn't loved having him here. Regardless of the disgusting images of Sydra and him floating around in the back of my mind, I was happy to have him close to me again.

I smiled and took a sip of the tea out of politeness. He could see my nerves dancing the jive, and there was no hiding it. Though I'm often quiet, I've never learned to hush my body language. He knew my every facial expression, every mannerism, and it gave me away to him every time.

"I can always tell when your mind is somewhere it shouldn't be by the look of your hands. You pick at the skin around the edge of your thumbs until they're all red and raw. The way you've been at it, I'm surprised you've got any thumbs left," he chuckled.

I looked down at the bloody corners of my nail beds and smiled, glad he noticed such small things about me. It was a terrible and gross habit, but I was happy for him to know me that well, even so. Leave it to me to feel endeared by gnawed fingernails.

"I'm worried about her, Vanse. I keep picturing her sitting in her cell alone and scared...worse things than that, actually. You don't want to know the places I've been going in my head. I mean, she could end up in the— "

"I don't want to think about it J.L.," he cut me off. "We've talked it to death, and it's doing no good. We don't know what's comin'...there's no way of it. We just need to be in the moment, where we are right now. We have to live our lives. We can't help that she's in there, but we're wasting our God-given days away thinkin' about it out here. We get a certain number of times to open our eyes in the morning. Do we want it to be this every day?"

"I would think you'd be worried sick about her," I replied a little bit coldly.

"I am. But I've learned a lot over the past few years. I spent a lot of time trying to hide, myself...you know, after the war and all. Eventually, you have to face reality and find little pieces of happiness again just to make it through. I don't want to see anything bad happen to her anymore than you do...but I'm more worried about how you're doing. You can't weigh 100 pounds right now."

"Me? Why are you so worried about me? This whole thing is my fault. It's on my shoulders, and she's paying for it." I looked at him hard.

"That's not remotely true, and you know it, J.L. She's the one who let him back in this house, not you. Sid Bumgarner would be alive and well right now if she hadn't insisted and damn-near begged him to stick around when he showed up after the funeral. Had I been here, that wouldn't have happened..." he trailed off and got quiet, guilty that his effort to avoid my sister had kept him away.

"Now you're the one blaming yourself," I answered.

"Well, the truth is we all make mistakes. I would have been there to stop the whole damned thing if I hadn't been hiding from *her*...I acted like a little kid, and we all paid for it." He paused and turned to me, "About that, J.L., I-"

"You don't have to," I interjected. "I don't blame you for it. Any man would have gladly traded places with you that night. Let's just not do this, alright?" I started to fidget with a loose thread on the sleeve of my sweater.

"I need to get this out, J.L.," he said quickly. "I've been wanting to for a while now, and I mean, with everything the way it is, I haven't gotten around to it. We never talked about it, and it's been this huge elephant in the room just starin' at us."

"You don't owe me any explanations, Vanse. You don't have to justify your private life to me. We're friends." I tried to squash the topic.

"Being with your sister was a mistake," he continued anyway. "I'm not going to lie to you or insult you by acting like I didn't choose it. Did I want her? Absolutely. I wanted her, and...and I gave into it."

"Ok, great. Dinner?" I answered quickly and tried to stand up.

"I'm not finished, J.L." He took me by the forearm, just enough to stop me from moving. "I regretted it the second it was over. Then I acted like a pansy and didn't come back here to be with you after you'd just said goodbye to your Mother. I wasn't here when I shoulda been, and bad things happened because of it. I just regret it all. I wish I'd never touched her. It's the truth, and I need you to know that."

"How could you regret that? Don't patronize me,

Vanse. At least don't do that." I could feel my nostrils flare with anger, "You say you don't want to insult me, yet you're saying you wish you hadn't slept with a movie star for cryin' out loud. Don't apologize because you feel sorry for me because I'm not her. That's what you're doing. I don't need that from you of all people. You've always treated me like a normal human being, and now you feel bad for me too. Newsflash, Vanse, I'm glad I'm not Sydra *Parramore*."

"I don't feel sorry for you because you're not her, Jimmi-Lyn." His voice was stern now. "I'm sorry because it was wrong. It was wrong all together. It was wrong because I—"

I stared into his hard eyes. He had more to say but stopped himself from saying it. He ran his hands through the sides of his hair and looked at the ground. I could see sweat beginning to form at his temples, and his breathing had picked up pace.

"Because of what, Vanse?" I dared.

"This ain't the right time, J.L.," he whispered. "Let's just settle down a minute."

"For what?" I pressed him, finding some courage in the madness of the moment.

"J.L.—"

"You said it yourself, Vanse. We don't know how this is all gonna shake out. We just have right now. We don't know the future, so if you got somethin' to say, you'd better just go ahead and spit it out because I don't know what I've got time for anymore." For the first time, I felt that I had no patience for bullshit. I felt like I only had space in my head for what's real, and suddenly, I could not stand the way he was beating around the bush.

"J.L.," he paused and looked me in the face, "you know why it was wrong with Sydra."

I raised my eyebrows and threw my hands up prompting him to enlighten me. I was showing a side of myself I'm not sure he'd ever seen. I outright confronted him about his emotions, too fed up to be embarrassed about it.

"It was wrong because of you." He finally said what he'd been thinking, more matter-of-factly than I had expected.

"Because you know how I feel about you," I responded candidly, unable to believe I'd just said that even in my brave moment.

"No, J.L., it was wrong because the way *I* feel about *you*," he said shaking his head at me. "I realized it...at the funeral. That's why I finally came over here that evening. I had to talk to you about it all, and I wasn't sure you'd want to hear what I had to say. I knew it had hurt you, and more than anything, I wanted to try to fix it somehow. But when I got here, everything had already happened. It was just this horrible, shocking scene. And since then, there has been no time to have this conversation. It's just been all about what's going to happen to Sydra. I mean, I didn't know if it was even fair of me to walk up to you right after your mama's died, with your sister in jail for murder, and be like, hey, I want to be with you by the way. *Deal with that too.* I didn't know how to handle it, so I didn't, not till now."

"You don't want me," I replied in a whisper, my tone annoyed, though I'm not sure what my exact emotion was. I always expected to be thrilled if this moment ever came, but now that it had, I just felt like I had nothing left to give.

"Yeah, J.L., I do." He put his rough hand on top of mine and tried to look me in the eye.

Tears welled up in my eyes when I looked back at him. This is what I had imagined for years, what I'd hoped for my whole life. I wanted him to want me the way I wanted him, but now that he was saying it, I couldn't believe it. Why would he? After all, he knows - and the things he still doesn't - why would he want to be with me?

"Vanse...Vanse, I'm not beautiful...I can't give you children. I'm—"

"You are beautiful, J.L.," he stopped me, "and I've always thought that. I know all the reasons you think you're not, but you are...inside and out. I don't care about all the things that have held you back from loving or letting somebody love you. I don't care about the things that kept you unable to be honest with yourself about us. It took a long time to be honest with myself about it, too. I was stupid for a really long time. I could have been loving you for years. Really, J.L., I have been. I made a huge mistake that I'll always regret. But even when I made it, it was you that I loved. I'm so sorry."

"Vanse." I squeezed his hand. "You and I would have been so perfect for each other in another life." I could feel tears prepping for war in my throat.

"Why not this one?" he challenged me.

"Too much has happened. I'm really messed up about a lot of stuff, Vanse...you don't need my burdens. You don't deserve them either." I shook my head and pursed my lips. "Then, there's Sydra. The fact is, you *have* slept with my sister, and I think she's in love with you. Always has been. She's in jail facing murder charges because of me, and I'm here trying to pretend I'm not in love with the one man she's been mad about her entire life. You were right to begin with, Vanse, the timing is so far off. It's like a cruel joke from Fate."

"How am I supposed to let you make this mistake, J.L.? You're just gonna throw our chance away because of things other people did? Just like that? Are you not even gonna consider just being *happy* with me? Are you hell-bent on giving up before you try?" He fired questions at me like an enemy soldier.

"Vanse, I think I have to." I was still squeezing his hand. "I think I have to leave us sittin' on that beaten up plow in the middle of the field under that warm tobacco sun that shined on us all summer long. I'm glad to put us right there in that world and stay forever with you in it. But who we are, right here, in this screwed up house," I paused and looked at my surroundings, "I think those people used up all their hope already...and Vanse, well, there's still something else you need to know about the day Sid died." I felt myself start to tremble.

Before I could speak again the ringing phone sliced through the space between us, jolting me out of the courageous place I thought I'd found to tell him the one thing I'd still been hiding for months now.

"I'm gonna grab that," I whispered, knowing my moment had passed.

I made my way around the corner, into the kitchen, and grabbed the phone on the fifth ring.

"Hello?" I answered half out of breath.

"Yes, is this Ms. Brawley?"

"It is," I replied.

"Hi, Ms. Brawley, this is Officer Jenson with the North Carolina Department of Corrections. I'm calling in regards to Sydra Bumgarner."

"Yes, sir. Is everything alright?" My heart started pounding the second he said *officer*.

"I'm afraid Ms. Bumgarner has had what seems to be an anxiety attack of some sort, a series of them, actually. We checked her out, and she's ok, but she is demanding to see you before continuing with her evaluation sessions. Normally we don't give into this kind of thing from inmates, but she was very distressed and is at a bit of a stalemate with everyone. Nothing moves forward until she gets through this part and she won't say another word until she sees you. Her doctor suggested we reach out to you. It's ultimately your decision to come or not."

"Ok, yes, I—I'll be there in the morning. Does that work?" I answered hurriedly and frantically.

"Yes, Ma'am. I'll let her know we reached you. I'm sure she'll be glad to hear it."

"Yes, thank you, Officer." I hung up the phone and paused, looking at the receiver for a second. I wondered what could have possibly sent Sydra into such a down-grade, and it scared me.

"What is it?" Vanse asked leaning in the doorway.

"Something's happened with Sydra. She had some sort of breakdown or something," I answered rushing past him down the hallway into the bedroom.

He trailed behind me. "J.L., stop. Why did she have a breakdown?"

"I have no idea, Vanse," I answered rudely, too concerned for questions right now.

I threw a brown-carpeted suitcase on my bed and began throwing clothes into it with no organization whatsoever. Tears were streaming down my face as I tried to wrack my brain as to what she had said or done. What had made her lose control? What all did the police know now?

"You think it's a good idea? You involving yourself with this?" he asked sincerely.

"Vanse, I am involved in this. I am 100% involved in this already," I snapped.

"I'm just saying. You're no psychiatrist. Maybe it's best you let the professionals handle her."

"I'm going, Vanse. I have to," I replied while rummaging through my tiny closet.

"Well, I'm going with you. No arguments. I'll take you down there," he said protectively.

"Fine." I didn't refuse because I knew I needed the ride. My pathetic car would barely make it across town.

I was rushing about the room; throwing items everywhere in near panic myself. Sydra could have just changed everything without me knowing about it. I had to talk to her. We had to revisit that day even though we said we wouldn't.

"J.L., stop a second." Vanse grabbed my arm, twirling me around to face him. "What did you have to tell me before? I want to know."

"Vanse, I can't right now, please." I jerked away from him.

"J.L., you've never lied to me before. You gonna start now?"

I looked at him sincerely, starting to become aware of my attitude. "If you'll just let me get packed, and promise me the ride no matter what, I swear I'll tell you everything."

CHAPTER 17

DR. GARRIS

I try not to take my cases home with me. I try my best to leave them at the office or in a textbook, but I never let them follow me back to bed at night. I made a choice early in my career to not haunt myself outside state-governed hallways. That's just asking to become a patient one day. I could easily drive myself mad if I let go too much, then I might find myself as the shiny red apple of Rathburn's ill-intentioned eye.

However, I broke my rule today and took Sydra to my house. I brought her right in the door with me and let her watch me change into my running shorts and tennis shoes before heading back out the door. I let her jog right along beside me, through the oak trees, and down by the cool Eno River. She was fully in my head.

Psychology is one of those fields that tend to get personal if you aren't careful. We hear everyone's horror stories and dirty little secrets. We're here to listen to the things that were never meant to be talked about; the things nice families swept underneath rugs or hid behind the blackout curtains. We drag those things out of the not-so-safe corners of the mind kicking and screaming to become the sounding wall for every filthy, unhealthy, or just plain ridiculous detail. When that happens, if we aren't cautious enough, the compassion can overthrow the logic...or worse, *passion* overthrows the logic.

In the younger days of my career, the war stories would regularly come together and perform a tap dance routine for me every night. Every vile thing a pedophile had ever told me or every gruesome detail of a grim murder became a disgusting, clamorous song I couldn't get out of my head. I considered changing fields more than once because of this. I seriously looked into being an accountant at one point, so much that I even signed up for the course. Nothing there to fear except paper cuts.

However, as the years went on, I was able to learn to separate myself from most of it. I don't know what I did to accomplish that. There was no magic recipe that helped me turn my mind off. There wasn't a song serene enough, a lover pleasurable enough, or a book good enough to drown those things out. Like everything else in life, it just took practice and patience. I learned to shut off my mind by willing it to do so, and until recently, have been pretty successful at doing it. Perhaps my ability to shut off my mind allowed me to work with some of the most difficult and dangerous criminals in the area. I could stand listening to the details that the other doctors couldn't. I could handle the insults, the lies, and the threats. I easily saw past whatever the inmate was spewing and could get to the marrow of who they were every time. Plus, I had no patience for paper cuts...

I've met far more sinister people than Sydra Parramore, and have heard many more disturbing details in other cases. Truthfully, I might have let Rathburn take a stab at many of them with that ice pick he's grown so fond of. There's something off in this one, though; something that I need to figure out, but I don't know how. Something tells me this woman needs help. I can't see her with her finger wrapped around a cold trigger. I see her wiping blood splatter off her disheveled dress. I see her as not the *perpetrator,* but as the *victim.*

It seems it would be such an easy thing, figuring out what makes Sydra tick. There's no way this woman is as complex as she's trying to appear to be. I think that's why it keeps coming home with me...I don't understand her, though I don't know what there could possibly be that's so hard to grasp. I don't know what is so special about her, and why I fear for her safety so much.

I've met smarter criminals, crazier ones, even more vain ones. Yet, it is this poster girl from a tobacco town in the middle of nowhere that has me guessing. I don't know how to tell her that if she doesn't end the games, Rathburn will find the right people to convince into letting him use her as his personal lab animal. That's why I had to bring her home with me. I know deep down that I'm the only one who can save her. It may not be my place, but I can't help but feel like it's my duty.

Maybe her fault is that she *is* so much different than

the others. She's not as scary or as demented. Therefore her *quality x* that escapes me now, has been left out of the college textbooks. She's a real person with a Hollywood ego that makes her larger than life. But, perhaps figuring her out is not as involved as I initially thought. Maybe she just wants to be that simple Tobaccoville girl but thought she couldn't. Perhaps, I'll just stick to the facts, observe what she shows me, and stop trying to fit her into the typical molds. She's unique. My professors taught many courses on the bent minds of hysterical women, but they never taught one on Sydra Parramore. I don't know if it would have been hard to grasp, but unprecedented. Whatever she is, is certainly hard to find...like a shiny, radiant stone hiding in the grass. I feel like it would be so easy to see if I only knew it was hiding there.

What stands out the most about her is that she's trying to manipulate me. That *was* easy to see, but I don't know why she's doing it. It wasn't to get out of a conviction. She freely admitted she killed her father, though she doesn't want to discuss the reason. She doesn't care if I see her obvious guilt, so in her attempts to control me, what is it she doesn't want me to see?

In most cases, the patient's motives are the first things I see. I know I'm trying to be steered towards an outcome of the criminal's liking, which they normally reveal very quickly for the sake of their goals. She has yet to let me in on what her hopes for herself are. When I ask her, she evades the subject. Perhaps she cannot yet decide if I'm an enemy or an ally of hers. Clearly, I've decided for myself to be on her side, but I think it would be a mistake to let her in on that. I know I should be neutral, but I'm human. I have science, but I also have instinct. It's the latter that I cannot deny, telling me to fight for the woman currently trying to wield me so skillfully.

Another thing about Sydra that is just remarkable to me is her ability to remain detached without appearing *incapable* of emotion. I'm certain she could pass a polygraph even if she claimed to be the reincarnate of Joan of Arc, but I'm also certain she could cry real tears while doing it. Maybe that's how she's found success as an actress. However, this skill is of no help to me. It just muddies the waters we're treading. At least with most murderers or other criminals I deal with, I would know how despicable they were, or how broken. I knew why they did or did not do whatever they'd been accused of doing. I had the explanations. I knew where they fell on the sanity scale. With Sydra, I would think I had her figured out, and then she came out with something else. I couldn't tell her lies from the truth, though I knew I'd been receiving both from her. Didn't she see that she kept walking on briars while I've chased her around, holding her shoes?

There were a few things I did know about her, and that's what I needed to focus my attention on. She wasn't crazy, but she wasn't well. She's most certainly not a sociopath, though, I'm 100% percent sure she's a narcissist. I read Cleckley's, *The Mask of Sanity* from cover to cover when it was published about six years back. Sydra fits a few of the personality traits of an anti-social, but no more than three of the sixteen. She felt real emotions, too much for psychopathy, and her vomiting from a simple upsetting thought proved that today. She was highly self-centered, far beyond the average individual. She viewed everything in the universe as an extension of herself. She evaluated things, like most people, as to how they pertained to her personally. However, unlike most people, she thought the rest of the world was on board with it as well. She thought that somehow we're all here to serve her.

I believed she admired everything about herself, including her flaws. If there were any attributes about herself too painful to address, she chose not to acknowledge them. From our sessions, it seemed to be the same with memories. She would be unlikely to bring up something she considered particularly painful. That could be why we hadn't had a breakthrough and why she has yet to supply her motive. I wished I'd stuck an ink pen in my shorts pocket so I could have written that down. I'd have to remember - *find a way to sift through her memories.*

I knew how close we were today - if I'd only had a few minutes more. She began panicking when she lost control. Without control, two things happened. First, she couldn't decide where to go next, which caused her great anxiety and created a space where she may reveal secrets. Second, she was no longer the star, which to her, might be worse. The egomania.

Still, I wouldn't peg her as the sort to *kill* out of her narcissism. She needed the admiration of others far too much to keep her world spinning. She thrived on getting praise and having followers. If she killed out of narcissism, she'd be downright giddy about the media catching wind of it, but that idea terrified her. She had an entire team of people bending over backwards to keep the "recovery spa" facade up. She wanted to be loved and wanted those who loved her to be awe-stricken. This included her father. She wasn't the kind of narcissist who liked negative attention. She was only interested in the admiration. She was the child who did yo-yo tricks for praise, not faked a twisted ankle.

Could she have killed her father out of anger or jealousy, perhaps? Did he not admire her enough? Was she somehow jealous of his unsavory affections for her friend, Maggie Morgan? All probable yesses, but she wouldn't kill over it. That would eliminate her chance of ever 'winning' her father over again. Then, she loses the contest, and she considered herself a competitor of everyone.

There's also the Jimmi-Lyn clause. There's something that involved her sister that she still hasn't told me. Could she somehow be the reason this all happened? If I were a betting man, I'd say Jimmi-Lyn incited the murder in some factor, but that's only based on a hunch. *Why? Why did she do this? Think Garris.*

I made my way back to my front porch steps and back through the door of my rustic ranch-style house. I bent over and put my hands on my knees to catch my breath for just a moment. I stood up and rubbed my temples too hard for it to feel good, hoping to rub Sydra right out of my mind, if only for a few minutes.

I shuffled, almost like a sleepwalker, to the bedroom and pulled my t-shirt and shorts off, throwing them on top of my dark wooden dresser. I looked in the mirror at myself standing there in nothing but tube socks and my own sweat. I only had the bedside lamp on and could barely make out the stray greys in my chest hair.

I thought I still looked pretty good at 43. My abdominal muscles hadn't gone into hiding yet thanks to my five-day-a-week jogging habit. It could be a lot worse. Some of my colleagues who were younger than me looked like British attorneys with bright white wigs. As I looked myself over, I couldn't help but wonder what Ms. Parramore thought of my looks. I pictured her pinned up on my wall, looking straight at me. She never had been, but I'd seen her on many others in my day, in bars and barracks. I imagined her bedroom eyes gazing down, looking over her shoulder...and of course, directly down her nose.

"Stop it," I said aloud, shoving the top drawer of the dresser shut with force.

I turned away from the mirror. Did she know she was in my head? I could picture her throwing her head back and laughing before blowing a mouthful of cigarette smoke into my face. She'd then say something she considered to be fabulous and watch me squirm on the end of her hook. She'd love this far too much, my wallowing in the confusion she'd made. Right now, I felt like she was a ghost in the room with me, so much so that I shivered.

I pulled up my blue striped pajama pants I retrieved from the drawer I'd just slammed and sat down on the edge of my neatly made bed. I reclined onto my down pillow, and took a deep breath in, letting it back out nice and slowly. Getting control of my breath would trick my body into thinking I'm relaxed. I sat my glasses on my oak nightstand beside a bottle of nasal spray and shut my eyes, though they fought me to stay open a few minutes longer, clearly having joined the Army O' Sydra.

I allowed myself one more question about the enigmatic Ms. Parramore while I lie there in a state nearer to unconsciousness than lucidity. What was it she was trying to convince me of? That's where the answers always were. That's where the lies would be. Sometimes they're revealed simply because they're dodged. Whatever people tried to convince you of, just the opposite was usually true. It's much like how a magician convinces his audience of his mind-blowing feats. He doesn't trick so much as he redirects and shows the viewer where to look with distractions and theatrics.

I knew Sydra was trying to convince me she was unshakably confident. *Lie.* She tried to convince me she was very different from her mother. *Lie.* She tried to convince me I was in charge...*another lie.* She had the power, and I don't know how or when I gave it up. I could feel my handle on her slipping away more than ever. I'd brought her home with me for chrissakes. I was laying with her right now, letting her have the run of my house. I half expected to look up and see her prancing around pantless in one of my button-down work shirts.

I shook my head at myself and turned the lamp out. I settled down under the covers of my normally lonely bed, far too aware that Sydra Parramore was the only woman in it with me at the moment. I shut my eyes and tried to nod off, emphatically deciding not to let her back in my head for the night, certain I'd win the struggle this time.

I imagined myself staring out at the ocean while listening to waves bounce back and forth on a moonlit beach, the ebb and flow of the tide. I let my breathing join in the sea's chorus, and could feel my mind beginning to sway with the current. I began to let go and thought for a second my new nemesis was finally leaving me for the evening.

I danced in that area between dreams and reality for a while. I thought I'd found peace, and could have only been mere seconds from dozing off when I startled with a force that shook my bedframe. I sometimes dream I'm falling from buildings or ladders; that's what this felt like.... yet a little bit different. It hit me like a ton of bricks, real bricks, present. It wasn't a dream that scared me awake, but a revelation....the one I'd been hunting this whole time.

Sydra popped into my mind for her last encore, and I thought of one more thing of which the lovely young actress was trying to convince me. She was never for a second trying to convince me of her innocence, but always of her guilt. And she's been trying really, really hard.

CHAPTER 18

JIMMI-LYN

The morning was disgusting. It was raining so hard Vanse could hardly see out of the windshield of his Ford pick-up truck. I tried letting the downpour lull me to sleep, but it was too much. There was no charming pitter-patter on the glass; it was more a brutal beating, but still the perfect theme music for my mood. The squeak of the inept wiper blades sounded off about every five seconds with a high note followed by a slightly lower one. When it all came together, it was like listening to metal colliding with steel. I got the image of sword fights and drawn weapons, which is kind of what I felt like surrounded me anyway...a war where Vanse, Sydra, Sid, and I come running from different corners into an open field pre-soaked in the blood of our fathers, only to smash together into one broken pile.

I tossed from side to side, trying to find a place to rest my head, but I couldn't catch a break. The inside of the cab was wet with rain and humidity, and the hairs that had fallen loose from my ponytail painted themselves to my face in a sticky mess. I felt restless and gross. I could feel the bottom of my thighs sticking to the damp, cracked, black leather that barely covered the lumpy foam cab bench. I *hate* that feeling. Every time I tried to move it sounded like I was walking on a tile floor with gum on the bottom of my shoes. I began to grow angry at the truck itself for being so unforgiving. I aggressively flopped over one more time before I just stopped wrestling with the musty cabin. Instead, I sat plastered to the seat, faking sleep, the moisture expanding by the second.

We were about 30 minutes outside of Raleigh before Vanse called my bluff, which was the reason I was faking sleep, to begin with. Until that point, he'd pretty much kept his eyes on the road. His body language didn't give away much, but I knew the wheels in his mind were working even harder than the ones beneath us battling the wet road. Sometimes silence is more stressful than commotion. Silence is mysterious and leaves one to wonder. I'd left him alone with his thoughts all morning, and I knew he now had a lot of unanswered questions.

"Are you gonna keep your end of the bargain, J.L.?" He finally spoke as though I'd forced him to.

I kept my eyes shut, hoping he wouldn't press it, even taking a nice deep breath for effect.

"J.L.," he reached over and nudged me, knowing I was awake. "Answer me. Sorry, but I can't let you out of this."

I yawned and opened my eyes slowly, really trying to sell my sleep ruse. I looked around faking confusion, and wiped my eyes with the back of my palm.

"You hear me, J.L.?" He knew I had. I was not as good of an actress as my sister.

I sighed and looked out of the passenger window. I didn't say anything at all for a few moments but figured I owed him something. I didn't know how to begin the conversation. I didn't know how to start to tell someone something I knew they didn't want to hear.

"I don't know how to find the words, Vanse, I really don't," I replied rolling my lips into a thin line.

"Well, you're gonna have to try," he replied more sharply than usual. "You've been keeping me in the dark about something, and I need to know what it is. Right now. I'm tired of the secrets. I'm tired of all of this crap, J.L." His temples throbbed. "It seems like something is always hiding around the corner, getting ready to jump out at me, and I'm over it. Let's just get it all out, right here. I'm tired of pussyfooting around dark rooms because I don't know what's inside of them." I noticed his country accent thickening with his frustration, like continuing to stir potatoes into a big heap.

A crack of thunder sounded somewhere in the distance, and I wondered how this storm could get any worse. A streak of sky-to-ground lightning flexed its muscles, daring me to question that again. The morning grew darker instead of lighter, and so did the cloud that sits directly over top of me all the time. I shook my head a little, as though I had nothing to say, but spoke anyway, the rain picking up speed to pace me. I had to. Vanse deserved the truth.

"After the funeral...when Sid showed up...."

"Yeah," he urged.

"When I saw him, I didn't know what to say or do. I was just so stunned. Sydra ran straight into his arms as though no time had passed at all, just shrieking and jumping like a five-year-old. It's like she didn't care that he'd walked out on our sick mother and abandoned her. As far as the other stuff...you know, with me...I don't know what she has or has not put together about all that. If she suspected anything, it didn't seem to matter," I sighed and shook my head, mainly at Sydra, "I thought for sure that one time she'd seen what was going on, but maybe I'm wrong. I thought she'd seen us through the darkness on the living room couch..." I shifted to face him better. "It doesn't matter, anyway. The point is, she was beside herself when she saw him standing there. She squealed and carried on. She just leapt right up around his neck."

"Yeah, and you said you passed out. And when you came to, you asked him to leave, right?" Vanse followed.

"Right. I was only on the ground just a few seconds. And I did ask him to leave. Almost immediately. I told him I thought his showing up was disrespectful to everyone involved, and that he should get out. I even threatened to call the police if he didn't get off my property."

"So, why didn't you call them?" Vanse asked in a way that made me feel accused.

"I was just so quickly overruled," I replied, feeling a little offended. "Sydra muttered something like, 'Oh pish posh,' and just blew me off and ushered him right into the house. I'd just buried my mother. I was upset...I..."

"It's ok, J.L.," Vanse softened up his tone. "Go ahead. I didn't mean to come at you like that."

"I just sat there on the porch swing for the longest time. I wasn't about to go in the house with him. I sat outside *my own* home listening to them laughing and exchanging stories. They were in there a couple hours, clanking dishes around, having a great time. I was waiting it out. I didn't feel like I had any other option. Plus, I'd just gotten my sister back. Maybe part of me didn't want to upset her either. I don't know. I convinced myself to let them have their time together, then just move on. I figured if I stayed scarce, eventually he'd go away, and it'd be over."

"Right," Vanse nodded.

I continued, "But things changed at some point. The laughter stopped, and the mood was just *different*. Their voices got louder, and they were kind of snapping at each other. I could hear them flat out arguing, but couldn't make out what they were saying. Sid's tone turned that familiar, ugly, just completely *sinister* way I am so used to. I got off the swing and put my ear to the front door, feeling like I was about to throw up. I still couldn't make anything out, but I heard Sydra start to scream and then dishes hit the kitchen floor. In almost the same instant I could hear feet scrambling around, and furniture getting bumped into." My heart was starting to pound as the beginnings of what transpired that day came flooding back to me.

"And that's when the scuffle started," Vanse added.

"Yes...but not the way you think," I whispered nervously.

Vanse sighed, "Just say it J.L., whatever it is, just tell me. You can trust me," he reached out and squeezed my trembling hand.

"When I went into the house, Sid had her by her throat up against the China cabinet in the hallway. He was kissin' all over her face like an animal and pullin' at her clothes. She was screaming and crying, snot and black mascara running down her cheeks. She was yellin' for me to do something, I mean the best she could...he had a pretty good grip on her. I just stood there kind of shocked for a second, unsure if I was watching her in the present or myself in the past. She was screaming for me to get him off of her, and I didn't know what to do. I knew first-hand how strong he was. And I—I remembered the shotgun inside the pantry door."

Vanse had pulled the truck over without me realizing it. He was looking at me hard and nodding. His face was getting damp with sweat, and his brow was crunched with confusion. He looked like someone just told him Pearl Harbor was bombed again. Maybe that's how he felt. In our small world, the things I was laying on him now were about as close as we could get. I was about to release another bomb on him, and I knew it was a surprise attack.

"I grabbed the gun and pointed it at Sid and told him to let her go. I was trying to just scare him into running out of there. I figured he would...I mean I was pointing a gun right at him. I assumed he'd let her go and then I could call the cops...but he isn't wired like normal people. He just barely paused a second, and chuckled at me the way you laugh at a two-year-old for trying to shave his face. It was like he thought it was cute how I was trying to stand up for my sister," I paused with the images of that day flooding my mind, almost drowning it.

"Keep going, J.L.," Vanse urged me quietly. "It's ok."

"Without letting go of her all the way he looked at me and said, 'Why, you jealous?' It was that disgusting, drawn-out, guttural voice I didn't think I'd have to hear anymore. He just sneered at me, looking at me like he knew I wasn't going to do anything. I kept swearing to him I would. The more I promised I'd do it, the more amused he became with me. He was laughing out loud... and his eyes...they were on fire."

Vanse still had my hand, and without letting go, slid across the seat, closer to me. I could see him swallowing hard and knew he was fighting off his emotions the best he could. I hadn't seen him cry since we were kids, but I remembered what it looked like. His lips were only slightly quivering, but I could see his feelings about to outplay his strength.

"I could smell the alcohol on him from where I stood about six feet away." I swallowed hard and pressed on. "It mixed with that scent that was just naturally Sid. It was so sickening....that cologne made up of sweat and cheap whiskey. I backed away a couple feet until my back was pressed up against the porch door. He just kept coming closer and closer, finally pushing me out the front door. I could still hear Sydra weeping from the kitchen floor where she was crumpled up in a little ball, her stockings ripped and funeral dress torn. Her crying had become more like hums and whimpers."

"Oh my God," Vanse whispered with his head down, more to himself than to me.

"When we got all the way outside he was still grinning from ear to ear, looking at me. It was a sick grin that changed his face entirely. I wasn't looking at a man anymore, but a starving wolf, all rabid and agitated. I was shaking the gun at him, my teeth chattering with nerves. He kept telling me I wouldn't do it, that I couldn't do it. He told me I would never 'shoot my Daddy' and asked me if I remembered how much I used to enjoy bouncing on 'Daddy's knee like a good little girl'. He was blatantly teasing me, daring me to go through with it. And he just kept creeping closer until I, um...I...I..." Sobs began coming out were the words should be.

"Until what?" Vanse whispered, looking into his lap, needing to hear the words directly from my lips.

"I tightened my finger around the trigger and could feel my heart beating in my fingertips. I didn't want to do it," I replied crying harder. "But he took one more step towards me...and...and it was over. I pulled the trigger. I shot him in the chest once and killed him right there. I did it, Vanse. It wasn't Sydra...it was me. I killed Sid Bumgarner." I broke down.

"Jesus, J.L.," Vanse whispered, unable to hold his tears back any longer.

"Sydra ran out when she heard the shot, and started screaming over and over how it was her fault. I was sitting there on the blood-soaked ground in some kind of half-daze, the gun in my lap. Those first few minutes after are still kind of foggy...more like trying to remember a dream more than real life. I know she took the gun from me and started frantically wiping it down with a kitchen rag Mama had stitched with little yellow daisies on it. I just sat there frozen in fear. She kept saying that no one had to know, that we could wipe the fingerprints off and get rid of him and we'd both be fine."

Vanse was still listening intently to me; tears streamed down his famously strong face. This was the worst part of telling him everything, seeing him like this. I didn't want to put my burdens on him, but I felt relieved to be able to say it all out loud for the first time. Carrying it almost ate me from the inside out. Finally telling him my secret this morning may have kept me from completely breaking into the shards of glass I felt like I already was.

I pushed on. "I got to my feet, and we heard the sirens in the distance. The neighbor kid was plowing in the field and heard the gun go off, even though he didn't see anything. He had heard all the commotion and called the cops...that's how they showed up. Sydra said it was too late and told me not to touch anything. She put the gun in her hands and stood over him right in the pool of blood. I asked her what she was doing and all she said was 'I'm Sydra Parramore. I'll get off. You won't.' And... and I let her do it. I didn't fight her or insist she give me the gun back. I sat like a coward and let her take the wrap for me. I let her soak herself in her own Daddy's blood and lie to the police for me."

I looked at Vanse, and his head was in his scuffed and stained hands. He was breathing hard. "You're not a coward. You saved the both of you, J.L. You knew far too well what was about to happen to her," he finally said. "Sometimes we do things we didn't think we ever could to protect what is good."

I knew he was thinking of the war. I thought maybe I had my chance to ask him about it, but then I thought of how I would feel if someone had asked me about this. I decided to let it go. This was about my conscience, not his.

"I shouldn't have let her confess to my crime, though, Vanse. Not for any reason. I've let this go so far now, and I can't undo it. I'm terrified," I confessed.

"You think she spilled the beans to that therapist?" he asked with the most serious look on his face.

"I don't know. I think it's possible." I was still sniffling.

"Well, we don't know for sure. When you get there, you keep your mouth shut. She probably just needs calmed down. If we don't show up, that'll look suspicious, so we do have to go. If I know Sydra like I think I do, though, she just needs a pep talk," Vanse reasoned.

"That's not the issue, Vanse," I responded. "The fact is, I killed a man and she's taking the fall for it. It's not right...maybe I should just confess the whole thing when I get there." I let out a labored sigh.

"You can't do that. Dammit, Jimmi-Lyn, she's treated you like shit your entire lives. She let your *rapist—*

forgive me for using that word— back into your house for Godsakes. You were defending her. She was right... it was her fault. You did what you had to do," he was shouting, scared and desperate.

"But, Vanse, she didn't pull that trigger. And she's my sister...and I do love her. I didn't want to do this. It just happened so fast, and I let it go on." I had gone from sobbing to screaming now too, feeling confused and frantic.

"She was right, though, J.L., she can get off. They'll fry you. If she hasn't blabbed, you see this through like you planned. You hear me!? I can't lose you!"

He grabbed me and pulled me closer to him. He wiped the tears off my face and traced his rough finger down the side of my birthmark as though it were endearing to him in some way.

"I don't know what's going to happen, Vanse. And I'm scared. I'm so so scared." I gave in and let him hold me.

"I can't lose you, Pretty Girl," he whispered and looked into my eyes.

"You see it all now, though. Don't you?" I asked.

"See what?"

"Why your timing was so off. Maybe it's me who will end up behind bars. That's why I pushed you away when you told me how you felt. I could be the one on trial, Vanse." I wept into his chest, breathing in his scent.

"We can't let that happen, J.L. Please, promise me you won't talk when you get there. Promise me!" He stared into my eyes waiting for a response, though I didn't have one.

He looked at me hard and took a deep breath in and out. He took my face into his hands and ran his thumb gently over my bottom lip. I leaned into him without hesitation and let him kiss me, letting myself have it, knowing I might not get the chance again. I was kissing him for the first time in my life, and it was incredible. Despite what led up to it, and how damaged everything around us was, it was pure magic in the fleeting moment, and it belonged to us.

He pulled away for a second, looked into my eyes and smiled. "That was worth the twenty-year wait."

"So worth it," I whispered back.

"I won't lose you, J.L., I can't," he said matter-of-factly.

"You have me forever no matter how all of this goes. You've always had me, Vanse." I rested my forehead against his and brushed my nose against his like an Eskimo.

"I love you, J.L.," he said and kissed me on the tip of my nose.

"I love you too, Vanse."

CHAPTER 19

SYDRA

I didn't think my episode with Dr. Garris was my first meltdown. I didn't think it was the first time new ideas mixed with old memories and confused me into a chaotic rant. I had the sneaking suspicion it happened before, in dark rooms behind closed doors, when the set is quiet for the day. I get the eerie feeling that I've had many breakdowns exactly like that in late hours of the night after the curtain is called. This feeling of panic, discontent, and disorientation. It's like a familiar old friend dropping in to say hello. Its wicked presence has been with me many times before...this perpetrator of mine that's infiltrated my life.

I have this image of myself back in California, pitter-pattering around my house that seemed so far away from me right now. I saw myself in my terracotta rancher on Roxbury Drive, wiping my camera face off after a long day of shooting. I could see my loneliness, as present as my own body, that I somehow never managed to recognize at the time. I saw the false eyelashes being pulled off, and the rouge rubbed away with a plush cloth from my vanity drawer. My hair was already set in pink curlers for tomorrow, and my favorite silk robe -the teal one with purple flowers- had been taken off the hook above the velvet chair in my powder room. It clung gently to my freshly bathed body like Spanish moss clings to an oak tree after the summer rains. I clutched the crystal stemware filled with Petri's California wine - the white, of course.

My heart pounded while voices from my past ricocheted off the sides of my mind. I sipped my beverage and drowned out the faces that went with the voices until I could no longer tell who was who. They were all here, though: Mama, Daddy, Jimmi-Lyn, Maggie Morgan, Vanse, even poor Dan McCreedy at times. Mostly, though, it's Jimmi-Lyn. I could see her terrified face, flailing limbs, and scrunched-up brow, though I don't know why I envisioned her this way. And it was a foggy vision at best.

I drank more as I started to sweat, lowering myself to the rose-colored chaise in my dark living room that sunk two steps down from the vaulted foyer. My hands drew in, but they released with a few more sips, and I found sleep wherever it happened, be it the bed, the loveseat, or even the floor. I think that's how most of my nights went back in California.

The guards reached me in the knick of time. Garris had almost managed to drag something out of me that I didn't even know was in there, not all the way at least. It's hard to admit to myself that I don't know what would have come out of my mouth if they hadn't burst through the door right when they did. Had the officers not wrapped their equally thick arms around me, and taken me to the nurse, maybe I wouldn't be in here alone right now. It scared me to know that. Control had been my most reliable weapon, and it was escaping me. I wasn't sure how I would get the upper hand back now. It wasn't just my rear end on the line, but Jimmi-Lyn's too.

I thought I'd been so cautious, so planned out. But when I started remembering Maggie lying so lewdly underneath my father, my mind became like a scrapbook full of faces, clippings, phrases, and fragments of the past. I saw the images scattered about in every corner of my mind, and they weren't good ones. I had trouble telling the real pictures from the made-up ones, and they were all terrifyingly loud with far-reaching voices. I felt like they used to whisper to me, but now they screamed. The happy times mixed with the bad, becoming a cloud of chaos set to circus music. Reality completely evaded me, and I felt like I was falling, reaching for branches to grab onto on my way down, all of them resembling rotten tobacco.

I'd let go of the steering wheel just long enough to run completely off the road I'd so carefully travelled, and Garris knew it too. Had I not finally thrown up all over the floor right in front of him seconds before those Heaven-sent guards burst in, it could have been over for Jimmi-Lyn and me. I might have started saying the things in my mind with no regard for how they would influence my case. However, my stomach spoke up and took over for my mouth, not allowing me to make that mistake. It lurched and turned and heaved until I was silenced. I'm almost certain I didn't give anything away.

There I was, an actress wearing nothing but a serial number and her vomit. I noticed how the guards avoided touching me where the sick had landed. I think they even felt sorry for me when they helped me get back to my feet. Their normally cement faces went soft, and they handled me like an orphaned kitten. I remember seeing an elderly man with a cane outside the door, hunchbacked and withered. He was about 85 if I had to guess, and didn't look like he was capable of tying his shoelaces. I'll never forget how he looked at me, while he, too, avoided getting brushed by my vomit-caked clothes. It was embarrassing what I'd so quickly become - another disgusting inmate. I was someone one the pitied now pitied.

The girl in the gold bikini had been swallowed up in this place. I'd become repulsive to the men around me and turned into someone that had to be "handled." I hated that almost as much as I hated the panic itself. There aren't many things worse than being undesirable.

I got cleaned up and tried to harvest a little dignity. I spent an hour being observed by a nurse with a sour look on her face in the infirmary before I was released back to my cell. I sat crumpled in foggy solitude, staring at the concrete ceiling on a cot dirtier than the one I slept on my first weeks in California.

I couldn't help but wonder if I'd come full circle.

Had I made it all that way, nearly 3,000 miles to another life, just to fulfill the sick destiny Carolina had planned for me all along? It was like the tobacco itself had it out for me and continued to reach out with its malevolent brown leaves no matter how far away I went. The crop considered me to be its little sheep gone astray and would never stop coming after me.

I became convinced whatever happened back home that I'd attempted to block, avoid, or just wish out of existence altogether had a heartbeat in this place, pumping venom instead of blood. It had infiltrated the roots of the entire nation, trailing me, sinking its teeth into me, and having me. The poison would find me no matter where I went, and I think I knew it all along. Whatever ruined us all had legs, and they were as lengthy as a granddaddy long leg spider's. They were so long that they could touch me anywhere, but when they do, it's only for a second. They just stroke me long enough to make my hair stand up on a perfectly sunny day, and linger only long enough to let me know they were there, which makes whatever it was awfully hard to identify. Whatever trailed me so cruelly, for so long, had done so slyly. It wasn't like something I was a close companion with. The memories, the secrets, the toxins...the various parts of the monster...they were more acquaintances I recognized when they passed me by, out of the blue on a lonely street corner. I'd just get a flash of them here or there, only recognizing them when they showed up, which was always unannounced and sudden.

It turns out what I am is owned. I am owned by

where I came from, and I don't know what that says about my sanity. It may not be a matter of sanity, but circumstance. Maybe my bad past was a matter of nature, something I was born with, or born to. I told Dr. Garris in our first session that Jimmi-Lyn was the one born stained, but I've started to think it was me. Her blemish was only on her skin. It wasn't raised, couldn't be felt, it emits no odor. It was a harmless illusion at very best. I knew my tarnish hid in my veins just like Sid's and is everything *but* visible to the naked eye. The ugliness lived just beneath the surface like the devil himself, seemingly in another realm too far off to hurt anyone. In reality, the beast was but millimeters away, in striking distance of everyone and everything around him.

Maybe that venom I blamed on Tobaccoville lived inside me. Perhaps I was the epicenter, the cesspool, the reason, the *source*. Maybe Jimmi-Lyn's father didn't curse her at all, but mine cursed us both. Perhaps it is Bumgarner blood that ran through my father and me, that spilled like permanent red ink onto Jimmi-Lyn. If she is foredoomed, it is the two of us that did it to her, and not because we're beautiful. Bewitching? Maybe, but most certainly not beautiful. Maybe it was the Bumgarner in me all along; maybe I poisoned the tobacco myself.

"Inmate," one of the guards called from outside my cell while I revelled.

I uncurled from the fetal ball I was lying in and took the pillow off my face. I adjusted my matted eyes from the dark corner of my cell and looked outside towards the light where the voice came from. "Yes," I forced weakly.

"Just letting you know we were able to get in touch with your sister, Jimmi-Lyn. You'll be allowed a visit with her. She'll be here first thing in the morning." The guard clad in a blue uniform shirt spoke through the steel bars.

"Thank you," I croaked hoarsely before returning to my womb-like position.

She would be coming to my rescue once again. Just like when I was five years old and had fallen off a bike. I'd become hurt and hysterical, calling her to my side. Jimmi-Lyn rushed to pick me up when no one else would. She'd come to help me back onto the seat, holding on until I felt stable enough again. With her help, I would start to pedal and then she'd be able to let go, at least for a while.

As broken and half slaphappy as I felt now, I knew tomorrow would somehow be better because she was coming. I'd feebly roll over and let her fix me just like always. Maybe I could make sense of the puzzle pieces I'd strewn everywhere, and put my picture for Dr. Garris back together again. If I weren't strong enough, she would be. No matter our differences, I knew she completed me. I drink my sister in, I feed off her like an infant, and I'm powerful again. It's one of those things I know but would never admit to someone else.

If for no other reason, I had to pull it together enough to not let Jimmi-Lyn down. She'd always been there for me, and she deserved someone who could finally be there for her in return. I didn't feel an allegiance to many people; I knew how selfish and terrible I was. In my weaker moments, I didn't even enjoy it about myself. There's almost no one I felt patriotic towards...but to Jimmi-Lyn, from a dark corner where no one could see, I tipped my hat.

CHAPTER 20

JIMMI-LYN

My knuckles whitened as I took a strong hold around the rainy door handle at the North Carolina Department of Corrections. I had to do this by myself, though I was so very afraid. I had to wear a feigned brave face and walk into this building like I had nothing to hide. Wearing confidence was never my strong suit, but I had to do it today.

I hadn't faced Sydra since the day she was arrested. The image of her leaving in a squad car, handcuffed, and covered in her father's blood was still seared into my mind. Now I had to see her as a prisoner, and that might be even worse. I didn't want to do it alone, but bringing Vanse in with me as fragile as Sydra was, would not be a good idea. I doubted I'd have to fight him on it. She haunted him as it was, and seeing her would be like facing the dead. And that's what she needed to be to him. Some things just have to be dealt with solo, usually the toughest things, and this was one of them.

I took a deep breath in and let it out again, watching my chest rise up and down in the blotchy glass door.

I half expected the guards to charge me upon my first step through the threshold, tackling me to the ground to slam the cold metal handcuffs around my frail wrists. After all, isn't that what I deserved?

Instead, I walked in, a little sweaty, but moderately calm. I crossed paths with a mousy file clerk and made my way to a round desk in the middle of a stark, mostly empty lobby. It was a much different scene than I'd first envisioned. There weren't policemen standing watch for me with guns and nightsticks drawn, or official looking men bustling all around like I expected. In reality, the large room was nothing more than an open, boring space with ugly tan tile that smelled like the post office.

"Hi, I'm here to see an inmate...Sydra Pa- Bumgarner." I spoke quietly to the lady at the tall desk that hid her up to my collarbones.

"I.D. please." The pudgy middle-aged receptionist didn't even look up.

I fumbled with my patchwork purse until I found it, and presented the worn paper card to her. "Here you go, Ma'am."

She carelessly threw on some plastic drugstore reading glasses that matched her drab brown dress, pursed her reddish lips, looked at my I.D., then at me, before tossing it back. She handed me a badge and directed me to the third floor in a nasally southern accent that differed from my own. I thanked her and smiled slightly, clipping the plastic rectangle to the edge of my collar.

I made my way to the elevator, praying to myself all

would be well, still secretly fearing the receptionist had immediately alerted the force team that I was here. I expected to see the nose of one of their guns pry the cage-like doors back open just before they were able to shut all the way. When it didn't happen, I let a deep breath out and enjoyed the twenty-second ride like it was the Ferris wheel.

Once on the third floor, I went through what seemed liked a thousand more checkpoints, getting buzzed through here and patted down there. Finally, I was directed to a small square room where I'd wait for my sister to be escorted in.

I felt relief, a sick, selfish relief. I'd gotten away with it. Sydra hadn't given me up, or they would surely have me by now. I wished I had some way to signal outside to Vanse that I was ok. I could picture him out in the parking lot, stiff-jawed like he gets when he worries, tapping his good leg up and down like an assembly machine. I couldn't wait to let him know I was ok and see him let out the sigh of relief I just released.

As I thought of my good fortune, the guilt began to creep in. I was fine, but that meant Sydra was still charged with murder. She still had everything to lose, while I still had freedom - and Vanse. The tables had turned. It seemed I was the one with something to look forward to all of the sudden.

I heard the doorknob move, and when it swung open, I saw my sister stumble in without her typical grace. She looked, well, beautiful, even while she struggled in her shackles. She was somehow gorgeous, even with her usually perfectly curled hair falling straight behind her shoulders. Her skin, naked and pale, was flawless, not even a freckle. However, when I looked into her murky eyes, something was amiss. It wasn't her beauty; that was still there. She couldn't help but be gorgeous, that blessing has been one proven to stay with her. But, something else was gone that normally lived there, and I realized she'd broken in some way. Something had shifted inside her and was only visible when looking directly into her irises. Maybe there was a flaw of sorts, after all.

The guard sat her down in the chair across from me. It was so strange seeing her being manhandled like a common crook. Her chair was bolted to the ground, and the officer routinely rearranged her handcuffs to secure her to it. I took inventory of what she was wearing; I hadn't noticed it until she sat down. At first glance, I'd only seen her natural radiance like always, but now I saw reality. She wasn't a movie star or my sister in this place. Here, she was a prisoner, a faceless uniform with a number instead of a name. She was poorly dressed, distrusted, and nothing more than an object the state was in charge of keeping up with. Sydra Parramore was nowhere, and I wondered how long she'd been gone.

"You have 15 minutes, ladies." The chubby guard's voice sliced the silence before he walked out of the tiny room, letting the heavy steel door slam behind him.

The room was chilly. I immediately crossed my arms and hunched my shoulders. All the steel had somehow blocked the Carolina humidity from rolling in. I didn't think such a thing was possible, but this dump had achieved it. No wonder Sydra looked so lost. Who wouldn't look adrift after spending their days in here?

I darted my eyes around nervously and searched myself for what to say. I waited to see if Sydra was going to speak. I thought she was about to for a second. Instead, she stopped herself and said nothing. The burden was mine.

"How are you?" I asked her with the careful voice I would use to communicate with someone who doesn't speak my language.

"It's not a Swiss medical spa, but I'm alright. I guess." She moved her eyes back and forth as though there were other things to look at it the room. "I could *really* use a cigarette about now."

"Sorry, I don't have one," I answered. I was surprised she asked me this since I'd never smoked a day in my life.

"It's fine," she shrugged hurriedly and nervously.

I thought of asking her why she asked me to come, thought of making small talk about the rain. I had nothing to say to her, though, and 15 minutes was down to 14.

"Vanse's jacket." She pointed at me, her voice scratchy, but without inflection.

I looked down at the washed-out jean jacket I was wearing, forgetting I still had it on. I'd tried to use it as a pillow during the drive up and put it on when I woke up feeling chilly. I shouldn't have worn it in here. I knew how it was to feel like something was being rubbed in my face. I certainly didn't do it on purpose and had no idea what to tell her about Vanse yet. I didn't know what exactly there was to tell. What would I say when she asked why he didn't come in? Would she sense there was something between us? Things with him had just gotten complicated. I hoped, however, she didn't think my wearing his jacket in to see her was my effort to be cruel.

"Oh, he gave me a ride out here," I responded looking down at the jacket like I didn't know where it came from. "You know the shape my car's in. The truck got a little drafty, and he let me borrow it."

"Right," she responded, allowing us both to breeze past the Vanse subject for now. We had too many other things to talk about, though I wasn't sure what yet.

There was something with girth between us, a knowing, an uncomfortable silence that filled the air. I'd never felt so connected, yet disconnected, from my sister at the same time. Our bodies were there, the same ones that always had been, but we were different. Jaded. And we both knew it.

"I broke down on the therapist a little...well, a lot. I hope I didn't blow anything," she finally whispered, arms folded guardedly.

I just looked at her and shrugged, showing her I was ready to face the music if I had to. I reached across the table and took her hand into mine. She let me for a second, then remembered herself and pulled it away.

"I...uh," she stopped to swallow hard. "I remembered some things during my last session with Dr. Garris."

"Ok..." Now I knew how Vanse must have felt when I dropped my bombs less than an hour earlier. It was frightening in the dark.

"It shook me—they were like brand new memories that I'd never had before. I knew they'd been there for a while, though. It was almost like living with a person who stays locked in their bedroom all the time. You know they're there, but they're so scarce you forget all about them. Then when they come out, it's shocking, you know?" She looked to me for understanding, her face glazed with confusion.

I nod not knowing what else to do. Truth is, I had no idea what she was talking about. I never forgot anything, especially the hard things. There were times I wished I could have. I wondered if maybe they'd given her one of those new "drug tonics" I'd been hearing about. Maybe she was loopier than I realized right now. How bad was this episode of hers?

"That therapist...I don't know," she continued, "it's not like he said anything particularly great. But he fished those moments out somehow when he was stirring it all around with a big stick. It's like he sparked something up. And once it was lit, it was out of control and became this huge fire in my mind. Then I was upset, then—I don't exactly know what did it."

"What memories, Sydra?" I had to ask.

"A lot of little ones that don't matter...and then a few big ones that did. I think Garris knows something's funny. I got weird...messed some things up." She looked away and fidgeted with her bottom lip.

"What did you mess up?" I asked slowly.

Sydra started to cry, and her breath quickened a little bit. She had a look on her face unlike any I'd ever seen on her. She was on the verge of panic now and started patting at all of her pockets.

"Took my damn cigs," she mumbled.

"Just calm down a minute, Baby Sis." I made my voice soft, and added, "Just look at my face."

She smiled distantly. "That's what you called me when we were little girls...how awful you must think I am. You always looked after me, then the way I betrayed you..."

"What are you talking about, Sydra? You're in here accepting *my* fate. You're sitting here in a chair with my name on it. How could *you* betray *me*? I did this, Sydra, not you. I'm the reason you feel this way right now." I shook my head at myself, feeling disgusted I'd let it go this far.

"No...you may have pulled that trigger, but I caused this, and I can assure you of that." She looked me in the eye, still talking through tears.

"It wasn't your fault, Sydra, just like it wasn't *really* mine either when you get down to the nitty-gritty. You invited your Daddy in for supper. You didn't ask him to attack you, his own daughter," I stated this like a politician addresses a crowd.

Sydra began to cry a little more intensely as she shook her head, "No". I searched her face for answers and had a feeling I was completely in the dark about something. Maybe there were things I didn't know after all, and that scared me.

"I did invite it, though, Jimmi-Lyn. That's what you have to understand. God—-I'm so sick in the head...at least I know the reason why a little more now. Some things became clearer to me since yesterday. "

"What in God's name are you talking about? Stop speaking in code, please!" I tried not sounding frustrated, though I was - frustrated and frantic.

Sydra dried it up a little bit, lifting her cuffed hands up to wipe her eyes on her sleeve. "You know that part of the plan we discussed that involved telling Dr. Garris I left in a fit over Daddy having an affair with Maggie Morgan. That was going to plant the seed that he'd never been any good, wasn't the hero everyone thought he was. Then, we were gonna bring you back in later and say he attacked you when he came to town, and I shot him to save you."

I nodded.

"Hopefully, from hearing about how overlooked you were as a child because of me...then about Daddy with Maggie, and about him leaving Mama when she was sick, his latest "attack" on you would show the therapist that I had no choice. It was going to set up a chain of behaviors from him, but with one isolated event where I had to defend you, the weaker sister. I could claim self-defense or temporary insanity, and it would be perfect. The Maggie story was going to kick it off. Remember?"

"Yes." I nodded more hurriedly.

"The problem is with the whole Maggie clause." Her sniffles got heavier again.

"What about it? Why doesn't it work?" I ask, eyes wide, wondering if we'd somehow overlooked a hole in what I thought had been a carefully plotted story.

"I believed it was true. I believed for years that she *was* the reason I left Tobaccoville, Jimmi-Lyn. Now...that everything is clear to me, I guess you probably thought that story was a ruse...a lie to keep you out of everything till the very end. But I *actually* believed it. When we first went over what I would tell the cops, I believed that's why I really left. It wasn't just a story to me, it was real in my mind," she said this with a pitiful look of confusion on her face, making it look damaged to me for the first time.

I looked at Sydra and felt my mouth drop open. I was suddenly so sorry for her, realizing in that moment, that she actually *had been* unwell. My childhood had affected her, and she'd blocked bad memories, replacing them with new ones she could stomach. She'd created things in her mind from thin air, and then believed them to be true for years.

"The Maggie story...it happened....but, dear God, Jim, it was you!" She spoke through sob-hiccups. "It was you he had down in the living room that night. I'd completely made it something else in my head...but now I think it was in there all along, too, if that's possible. Somewhere, I had to have remembered just standing there and watching him do that to you. You didn't even ask for help. You just told me to go back to bed, because you didn't want me to see. You were crying, and he was drunk. You didn't want it, and he had one hand around your throat like he had around mine in the kitchen the day he died. I remember now. I just let it happen, then turned it into Maggie somehow in my head. I...I just didn't want it to be you." She was now inconsolable, and I was barely making out her words.

"Listen, Sydra, stop." I remained as calm as possible. "You didn't know how to deal with it, and your mind played tricks on you. You were just a teenager yourself. You couldn't have changed it." I grabbed both her forearms from across the table, shaking her slightly. "You couldn't have changed it. Ok?"

"But don't you see, Jimmi-Lyn? It doesn't end there, either." She bit her bottom lip that was now wet from the tears.

I moved my hands back down to hers, and this time, she let me hold them while she let all the secrets pour out of her. She was shaking, and her stark white fingertips were like ice.

"I was jealous," she said a little bit under her breath.

"What are you talking about?" I was still soft towards her, but confused.

"I was jealous of this 'special' thing he had with you. I thought if he loved me, or if I were pretty enough, he'd be having 'special' times with me, too. He didn't notice me like he did you, though." She shook her head. "And I wanted whatever that attention was. I could even sense the filth and degradation of it, yet I still wanted it in some way. It's so messed up, Jim," she whispered and looked like she might gag.

I didn't know how to respond to her. On one hand,

I was sickened by the fact that anyone could be jealous of the horror I went through...his sweat on my skin, his hot breath grazing my face, his *noises*. But, on the other hand, I kept thinking how seeing the things she saw, with no explanations of what was happening, must have let that ugliness claw into her, climb inside, and take up residence. It was something that coexisted within her, and she thought it was normal.

She was so little when it started. How could she have known anything was off? The story she turned into the Maggie Morgan episode was nowhere close to the first time she'd seen it happening. There was still a mountain of buried memories in her that she had no control over. Memories just sitting on simmer.

I don't know how I didn't see before today - just how mental she had become. She wasn't oblivious, but she was cracked, deranged. In her head, she decided that she was being ignored while I was getting 'affection'. She witnessed disgusting violence practically all the time before she was old enough to even make as much sense of it as I could.

I was always so adamant that Sid would never truly undo me. He ruined my body, my trust, and even my womb; but I had my mind. It couldn't be touched by any part of him. It never occurred to me that Sydra, with her healthy body, her innocence, and her willfulness, would catch the debris from the things that flew off me. She was in my eerie shadows, looking around the corners of dark rooms, left to try to *perceive* all that she saw. She'd done the best she could.

I knew she'd wanted to be the apple of her daddy's eye, always. I didn't realize the terrible reasons she thought she wasn't, though. The man everyone thought was so great, in her eyes, gave me so much more than he gave to her. She felt rejected, undesirable, and jealous. She didn't want to settle for being her father's paramour.

"I love you, Sydra," I managed, not knowing what else to say.

"Jimmi-Lyn...there's still more to this you need to know."

"It doesn't matter Sydra, whatever it is. We just have to figure out how to handle Dr. Garris and the police. You're as broken as I am, maybe worse. You don't deserve this. I want to tell them the truth now, Sydra."

"You can't do that, Jimmi-Lyn. Let me explain the rest to you because it matters. I know you just think I'm crazy now, but hear me out." She'd finally stopped crying, and her tone had gone completely serious.

I pursed my lips and gave her a relenting nod to go on.

"That afternoon when I let my father in the house, I picked that fight with him. At first, I just needled him, trying to get him to compliment me or notice me...exactly like a kid would do. I wanted him to give me some sort of approval in some way...*any* way. I mean, we sat talking for the longest time, and it had been years since he'd seen me. He didn't congratulate me on my career, or tell me I looked nice, or say he was proud of me, or anything. I tried dropping hints by going on about the glamour, and my upcoming projects, but it wasn't working. He wasn't biting, would hardly even speak at all...except to fire questions about you." She cut her eyes as if Sid were here in the room. "So, I started being horribly antagonistic, acting like a bratty child. I started going on at him about how he always showed you more attention. I was poking at him, asking him if he'd love me if I were prettier, or if I unbuttoned my blouse one more button. I told him he was just like all the other men in my life. It was so repulsive, the way I was acting, drunk or not. And I know that now. I just...I was somebody else in that moment. Here, today, I can't even believe I'm able to say it out loud...the way I was towards my *father*." She covered her face with her unmanicured hands, her nails now chewed to the nubs, matching my own.

I could hear how disgusted she was with herself as she spoke. I was shocked to silence. There was something very wrong with her inside that I couldn't fully understand. And she was right; it was truly disgusting, but also pitiful in every way. I felt nauseated by it, and still sorry for her.

"We were both drinking, and he started getting handsy with me, asking if that's what I wanted, askin' if I wanted a little 'taste of Jimmi-Lyn's medicine'. It was so lascivious, the way he was talking."

"I've heard him say that before. It must be a favorite." I closed my eyes and shook my head.

"It's like I could feel his words crawling over my skin like depraved insects. He started getting rougher, and then I realized it wasn't something I wanted at all. It wasn't the kind of attention I needed from him, even though it's pretty much what I asked for. I fished for a catch way too big for the boat I was sailing in, but it was coming straight for me anyway. I started struggling with him and trying to get away, but he was just so strong. The memories of 'Maggie' popped in my head. It was all so scary and happening so fast. Then you were there. You burst in, and you saved me just like that. You were so brave. I couldn't let you go down for it after what I'd caused." She spoke with water beginning to pool up in her lower lids again.

"I was less brave than you think, Sydra. I didn't have a choice. I was scared too," I responded as kindly as I could.

"I left you with your choice, Jimmi-Lyn. I'd all but demanded it. I couldn't let you take the fall for helping me while I was being attacked. And it's true. I did think the cops would go easier on me than they would you. I thought I could charm their socks off and get off just like that." She snapped her fingers. "I really didn't think it would even go as far as it has. That was before I remembered everything the right way, and cracked up in front of the shrink, of course." She rolled her eyes at herself before going on. "Now I don't know what to expect. But, what's important is that you see you shouldn't feel so bad about letting me do this. I knew what he'd done to you and invited him to do it to me. You stopped an awful thing I began. Why should you fry for putting out the fires?"

"Sydra, it still wasn't your fault. Sid is your father, and he didn't have to attack you, no matter how you acted. You're sick, and have some issues you're going to need a lot of help working through. I'm not so sure the truth isn't the only way now." My heart sank when I told her this, and I immediately thought of Vanse.

"Jimmi-Lyn...I need to do this. I don't want to go away for a long time, but I will if I have to for more than one reason. I need you on the outside. I need you to be ok."

"I need you to be ok, Sydra. You're still my baby sister."

"Yeah...you were like a mother to me, Jimmi-Lyn. And...and I love you for it...but I need you to give me a couple days. Please. Don't do anything yet. I'm only asking for a little bit more time."

I sighed deeply before responding. "I'll wait another day or two, Sydra, and let things settle down. I can't let you go to prison for me, though, or I will never forgive myself for it. You're right about one thing...that this all needs to be thought through. Acting rashly won't help either one of us. We need to both know what we're facing from this point forward." I put my head to my hand, feeling exhausted in every way.

"I know. I just needed to talk to you and get my head straight and needed to make sure you had the whole truth. I don't think anybody is on to anything as far as the details of it all. Maybe we can both have a future. Maybe one that even involves us together as sisters again. But I know that doesn't happen if we talk right now." Sydra sounded somewhat confident again, though I didn't trust it lasting for long. Everything I'd ever thought about my sister had just changed in a matter of minutes.

The guard burst through the heavy door about that time and motioned for me to wrap it up with the waving of his husky hand.

"Ok, Sydra, I'll be back in a couple of days." I kissed her on the head nervously while the officer looked on.

"I'll be here." She smiled sweetly, like she had as an infant. But now, she reached to me from behind very different bars.

CHAPTER 21

SYDRA

$\mathcal{I}$ felt lonely the minute Jimmi-Lyn let the chubby guard escort her out of the conference room. Our 15 minutes together had been only a moment, and she was gone. The safety I felt, and the short-lived invincibility I harvested, left the room with her. Now I was sitting cold in my own presence, wondering how to get the confidence back that I had when this all started. I wasn't me, well the me I actually *liked*, without my sister. I knew that for sure now. Jimmi-Lyn, with her frailty, and her artlessly painted skin, was the walking, talking house where my strength lived. It needed her warmth, her heartbeat, her survivorship. The further she walked away, the more I could feel it whither, and I knew it was possible that it could die.

The room had gone still, and I searched the quiet for something to cling to. I looked around at the blank walls, trying to find something new to stare at. *Anything.* It could have been a scuffmark from an officer's black-soled shoe for all I cared. I just needed *something* different, *something* that could take my mind anywhere else, and *something* that was maybe some sign of life. I perused the walls, the floor, and the table itself, but found nothing. Even the particles of dust and grime had gotten lazy, refusing to dance in the slanted sunlight that came in here at the same angle every day. The filth itself had stopped swirling around in an effort to find a home here in the crevices of this jailhouse. Even the dirt had given up. Settled.

I wondered why I was hanging on and where I was finding the last bits of hope I promised Jimmi-Lyn I still had inside me. The only thing I had to look forward to right now was having my cuffs removed from my sore wrists. I waited eagerly for the condescending guards to come back for me, to lead me back to my cell where I could lie down on my cot. Maybe, on the way, I'd see a piece of chewing gum stuck to a drinking fountain again. I thought there was a wadded up blue piece stuck to it a day or two ago; maybe today it would be green or yellow. That might be a treat.

Usually, this time of year meant putting on a pair of Duke shorts and grabbing a blanket to sit on before heading out to watch the fireworks display over Holly Canyon, not searching for color in spit-out candy. Independence Day used to be a time to celebrate freedom by drinking beer and eating sweets made from the *Betty Crocker* cookbook. Now it's just a time to long for that seemingly granted freedom again, to wish for the chance to see another sunset from the rail of the Santa Monica Pier, to hope to hear a panhandler's jazz song from his saxophone nearby. Independence seemed such a long way off for me. It might as well have been another life.

I shook my head and tried to not think of California. Though it might be the most alive place on Earth, it wouldn't comfort me today. It was just too hard at this point, a place *too* full of the color I so desperately needed in my life...so bright it hurts to look at. The good times no longer healed my heart; they taunted me. The laughs no longer lightened my mood, but instead turned around and directed their fun at me. My old life in the dry heat, on the glamorous side of a camera lens, wasn't hope anymore, but torture. It was like trying to look directly into the sun. It just sharpens, shines, and blinds.

Two months ago I'd been so sure I'd breeze in here, tell my little story, then go home. I thought I'd be back in my lawn chair already, sipping a French 75 with extra powdered sugar over cracked ice. I just knew I'd already be back to enjoy, for the first time, the kidney shaped pool I had built in my backyard over the winter. I'd have my script in hand, picturing myself on location in Palm Springs, memorizing the sassy lines written specifically for me that no one else could possibly deliver with the right fire. The gardeners would be clipping at the yellow rose bushes, trying to pretend not to eavesdrop, feeling special for getting a live sneak peek. I would glance up at them from behind my tortoise shell sunglasses with the sole purpose of making them nervous. Then, I would stand up and adjust my checkered red bikini - the one with the ruffles on the bra cup and at the hips. I'd set the script to the side for a moment to dive in the cool water for a much needed break. That's where I thought I'd be...

How did I *get* here? How am I *still* here? I could feel myself slipping, losing the charm in my voice, and forsaking the fury in my fists. I could see the set going dark, the clamor starting to hush, and the director yelling cut. I didn't know how, but this journey of mine was going to close, whether I was ready or not. I was no longer sure where I might be in the end. What I did know is that I felt like I didn't even remember how to get home, or if I had one at all. I couldn't just step out of my jumpsuit and back into my evening gown. Too much had happened. Even if I made it out of all this, I wasn't sure I could go back to California. I sure as hell knew I couldn't go back to Tobaccoville. I didn't know if there was a place for people like me. Maybe that's what that wise man who grew up just a couple hours west of where I did was feeling when he wrote those famous words in his last novel, the lines I remembered while a cold chill chased itself down my spine...

> "You can't go back home to your family, back home to your childhood...back home to a young man's dreams of glory and fame...back home to places in the country, back home to old forms and systems of things which once seemed everlasting but which are changing all the time- back home to the escapes of time and memory." -Thomas Wolfe

CHAPTER 22

JIMMI-LYN

Vanse and I made it back to Tobaccoville sometime in the late afternoon. The ride back was no more comfortable than the ride down had been, but I did manage to find a little sleep on the count of pure mental exhaustion. I didn't have it in me to try to process everything Sydra had said to me, and I refused to let her have my mind the whole way home. There was so much more going on with her than I had ever realized, and at times she had actually lost touch with the reality around her altogether. I didn't know what to do with that just yet, and I certainly wasn't ready to talk about it. The only thing I could think to do was just to shut my eyes and breathe. In and out, in and out. Eventually, it became a lullaby.

Vanse was quiet even before I drifted to sleep. I knew the morning had been hard on him, too, and we'd both dealt with the fact that we could have lost one another forever. Had Sydra said the wrong thing, that's exactly what would have happened. I would be the one behind bars right now, wearing the coveralls, praying for a miracle. Luckily, this time, she hadn't. Lucky for me, anyway. I think Vanse and I were both thankful for that, and it was enough for a win today.

When I came across the parking lot outside the jail, I saw Vanse sitting in his faded red truck with his cheeks puffed out, holding his breath. When he saw me, he blew the air out slowly, closing his eyes for a few seconds. He was just smiling at me, and he was alright again for a minute. I decided to hold on to that a little longer and let him do the same.

There was no point in talking about what's already happened or what might happen tomorrow or the next day. For now, Vanse and I both had to be comforted by the fact that we were given more time, however much or little it may be. There's no real way to find peace with the unknown, which was the only thing that lay ahead of us. I think that's why today, we didn't attempt to try. We had to hold on to our victories while they were still alive, with no way of predicting the shelf life.

When I woke up, we were about half a mile away from the house, and my stomach stood on its head. I wanted to be anywhere else...well, maybe except for where Sydra was.

"Ugh, I don't want to go back there yet," I said groggily, my eyes adjusting to the afternoon sun.

"Well, look who's finally up!" Vanse smiled at me and playfully slapped the top of my thigh.

I smiled back at him sleepily and immediately

thought back to our kiss earlier in the day. I was so grateful to wake up and see that face, more appreciative than I'd ever been for anything before. I scooted around in my seat to face him and offered him my hand, which he accepted instantly. I sat gazing at him when I realized we missed the turn-off to my house.

"Hey, where you going?" I asked glancing back at the rock-covered road we should have turned onto.

"You said you didn't wanna go home yet," he responded. "I thought maybe we'd catch us a little sunset. We're due one, don't ya think?"

My heart picked up a few paces as he hit the turn signal. I felt like I was about to go on a vacation. Although, I didn't know what that would be like. I'd never been on a real vacation before. I'd only left the state twice. Once I went to Chester, South Carolina with Sydra and my mother for my great-grandmother's funeral. Another time, I rode to the Virginia line with the neighbor to haul a few hundred pounds of sod and some farm equipment. I got to see another state and was paid five dollars for helping unload the trucks. I happily tagged along. It was a good day.

"Where we goin'?" I asked excitedly and bounced in my seat like a little girl.

"You'll see," he said steering around the hairpin curves.

I thought of all the places Vanse must have seen in his time with the Army. A back road in Tobaccoville probably didn't top the list. I wanted to know the places he had been, wanted him to describe them to me, and take me there in my mind. He never talked about it, though, which made me think maybe it's something I shouldn't ask about. Whatever he'd faced over there had overshadowed the brilliant green hues of the Pacific or the magic of the Japanese Alps. What I picture to be a fairy tale, I think may have almost undone him. Maybe I'd never ask. My curiosity isn't worth him reliving his sad stories. Maybe we'd told too many of them already. Perhaps I'll just let him keep his scar, and be his safe place.

"Vanse," I spoke.

"You'll see, I said. Be patient." He squeezed my kneecap excitedly.

"No...not that. Vanse, will you take me somewhere far away one day? Somewhere we have to go by a plane or by a boat?"

He looked at me with a wide grin, flashing his perfect teeth. "I promise we will. "

I put my hand on top of his that rested on my knee and looked out the front windshield. I felt like making big plans for a far away future meant that I'd have one.

"Hold on tight," Vanse warned, turning sharply off the main road.

The truck bounced up and down and shifted left and right, over the road that had become more like a creekside trail. I'd never been down this way in all my years in Tobaccoville. The makeshift route snaked around like a never-ending letter s. I thought maybe it just went on forever and we could follow it into another dimension; maybe somehow the road to Oz started in a little hollow in North Carolina that Vanse had stumbled across. Maybe the Emerald City was just on the other side of the hill in the distance, and I wouldn't need a boat or a plane after all. Maybe that's what I'd believe for today at least.

After a few more twists and turns, a clearing in the trees revealed a big open field with the widening creek running through the middle of it. It wasn't a river yet, but the water hurried by in just a quick enough fashion to make the place come alive. It seemed to give breath to the otherwise still woods on the outskirts of the fields and awarded the air a refreshing dampness.

The tobacco leaves were at their prettiest this time of year, lush, green, and tall. None of them had been harvested yet and stood proudly waving us into their abodes. They looked as though they had shown up just to dance for us and swayed together in perfect rhythm with the soft summer wind. It was the first field I'd looked at and appreciated in a long time.

"This place is gorgeous, Vanse. How did I not know about it?" I asked, my eyes beaming from edge to edge of the vastness that now fully surrounded us.

"It's a little hidden jewel. Not a lot of people know this land is back here. I worked the field once on a summer job a long time ago, before the army," he replied hopping out of the truck, his limp more noticeable than usual.

He made his way over to my side and helped me out of the cab, grabbing an old blanket from behind my seat. We walked along the edge of the lazy creek to the spot where it met the crops. The time of day had the little oasis set ablaze in a golden orange aura we became more a part of the deeper we walked. It was beautiful, aglow with the evening sun in every nook and cranny. We followed the sound of the gurgling creek to a dip by the edge of the water.

The sun narrowly found us in our secluded spot by the brook, but it managed to put the tiniest glow on our faces. We blended in with the things that became the muses of the sky, belonging to nature in this rare place, as whatever decoration it would have us be. I felt like a canvas for the fading rays, looking down at my illuminated skin. I smiled and stretched my arms out further, twirling in the open air, letting the Earth have me, feeling freer than ever. I could hear Vanse chuckling behind me while he spread the blanket out.

"I haven't seen you like this in way too long," he called to me, smiling from ear to ear.

I just laughed and twirled to the edge of the blanket like a ballerina before I collapsed onto it, laughing. Vanse slid in behind me and put both of his arms around my shoulders. I caught my breath as I settled against his chest and let out one of the first truly relaxed sighs I had in what seemed to be two forevers. He leaned into me, pressing his face into my hair, and breathed in. He loved me, and I knew it. I didn't want my time with him to be over. I knew I wanted a life with him and I gave in, letting myself dream about it. I knew it was dangerous to do that just yet, but in this perfect place, I couldn't help it. I wanted all the wonderful things I've always been scared to wish for.

"Vanse," I said.

"Yeah, Pretty Girl?"

"No matter what happens...will you keep me here?"

"What do you mean? I thought you wanted to go on boats and planes and rocket ships," he teased.

"What I mean is, can this moment right here, in this little place, always be where you remember me...if...if anything should happen?"

"Hey," he whispered, "don't talk like that. You're gonna be fine. Nothing bad is gonna happen to you."

"Promise me...please. I'm not trying to ruin how great this is...it's just something I need to know. So, promise me." I spoke softly, feeling a sense of reverence in this little dip in the hills that I now considered to be sacred.

"I promise," he whispered, turning me around to face him.

He took my face into his hands and kissed me gently on the lips. I pulled him closer to me, and he kissed me harder, not less tenderly, but more furiously. I ran my hands down his strong back and then returned to his stubbled face again. He moved his hands from my cheeks to my shoulders, pulling me as close to himself as he could once he got there.

I pulled back, catching my breath enough to whisper to him, "Make love to me, Vanse," without an ounce of shyness. I didn't know what tomorrow held, and I needed to be his in every way I possibly could. I needed him to be mine to the uttermost.

He hesitated only a second and looked into my eyes. He reached up and stroked my cheek, smiling, his blue eyes streaked with orange light from the sky. My life-long best friend answered me with his kiss and lowered me gently to the blanket.

CHAPTER 23

DR. GARRIS

$\int$ didn't wake up bright and early in the morning to confront Sydra Parramore about the things I thought I knew because I had never slept. Instead of finding rest, I found my notes from our sessions and began poring over them all. I'd become officially obsessed with finding the answers I needed.

I didn't catch any blatant lies or particular discrepancies in anything she'd said. What I did find was a woman who changed subjects rapidly, yet insisted upon herself at the same time. I found a highly divisive woman with a specific plan. I had her map now; I just didn't know quite how to read it. I knew I was close, though, slowly unlocking her legend and metrics. I was going to find her final destination, and I was hell bent on finding it today. She'd be surprised to find me waiting for her there. I couldn't help but smile to myself when I thought of this.

I kept glancing at the clock throughout the night, waiting for a time I could justify as appropriate enough to hit the road. I felt like the night was wasting my time and I was eager to hear the first bird chirp outside my window. This was a day like I used to have all the time early in my career but rarely enjoyed now. Excitement. Curiosity. Challenge. I suppose I had Sydra to thank for that.

I left Chapel Hill, heading slightly south-east to Raleigh while it was still dark outside. I watched the horizon swell with anticipation of the impending day for most of the way there. By the time I got to the prison, the sun had finally stretched its arms out nice and wide for me. It was going to be a great day. I had her this time, and I could feel it in my bones. At this point, there was nothing she could say to dissuade me.

I parked in the special permit lot and flashed my badge to the puny security guard at the faculty entrance. I was giddy like a high school senior on the first day of school. I felt like I owned the building this time, and pulled into the best parking space I could find as though it had my name on it. After I broke Sydra Parramore, maybe it would.

I hopped out of my black six-passenger Mercury with my brown leather briefcase and made my way through the gate to the entrance of the building. I could feel my feet moving in short, choppy strides, while I fought the urge to sprint inside. I blithely saluted the sleepy guard at the door, whistling *Yankee Doodle* as I walked by. He waved me in with a strange look on his face, and I made my way up the elevator to Sydra's floor, fighting a ridiculous smile the entire time. When I heard the ding, and the doors opened, I all but skipped into the hallway before making my way to the interview area.

"I need Sydra Bumgarner, please," I spoke, mono-tone, to another officer, hopefully hiding my over-zeal-ous disposition. The last guy had looked at me like I was nuts.

"You're her doc, right?" he responded in a country accent that told me he lived in the boondocks.

"Right," I responded, trying to stand still.

"Hang on a minute," he looked at his clipboard. "I think she's already in the conference cell. She just had a visitor."

"Just had a visitor? Who? Who was it? Was it that damn Rathburn!?" I demanded, realizing I probably came off a bit sideways.

"Easy, Doc," the balding policeman replied in an al-most taunting tone while he still fumbled with his pa-pers. "It was a Brawely. A Jimmi-Lyn Brawley," he looked up at me for my reaction.

Not at all what I expected. I wasn't sure if this was better or worse news than if it had been Rathburn. "Is she still here?" I asked frantically while trying to main-tain my professionalism.

"Uh, nah. Looks like she signed out about fifteen minutes or so ago." He referenced the paper with scrib-bled signatures on it.

Dammit, I thought to myself. I would have loved having them in the same room together to watch their behaviors. It would have been icing on the cake.

"Well, can you buzz me back?" I asked a bit disap-pointed while straightening my tie.

"Sure thing, Doc." He pushed a button and the barrier gate opened, a loud buzz echoing in the empty hallway.

I nodded a thank you to the guard and made my way back to Sydra. She was lying with her head down on the table like a disciplined grade-schooler when I walked in. She popped up when she heard the latch on the door open and sat up straight, assuming it was the guard to take her back to her cell. When I sat my briefcase down rather hardly beside her, she jumped a bit at the noise.

"Dr. Garris? I-I wasn't expecting you this morning." She gained a confident tone towards the end of her sentence. Typical.

"We need to talk, Sydra." I sat directly in front of her, crossed my legs, and stared her down.

"Ok." She swallowed visibly hard, and her pretty throat gave her away.

I was happy to find her a little on the nervous side, and she had every reason to be. Her little one-woman show, with me as the only audience member, was over. However, before she took her final bow, I had some things to go over with her. Without Rathburn peering through the observation glass, I could speak freely. Do things my way.

"I know you've been lying to me. I'm here for truth this time, Sydra." I got straight to the point, knowing tactics wouldn't work with her. She needed to know, in black and white, that I was on to her.

She laughed out loud, "Lying? I've admitted everything. I've been an open book. I've not once denied what

I did."

"You're trying too hard. That's where you've mis-stepped. If you're not outright lying, then you're leaving something out. I'm not here to try to pan for the facts like rubies in a mud hole. I'm going to be direct with you, and you're going to be direct with me." I spoke more sternly to her than I had before.

"I don't know what you're talking about." She rolled her eyes dismissively. Classic Sydra.

"I heard Jimmi-Lyn came by this morning. Why?" I trudged on.

"To check on me, of course. It has been two months. There's a holiday coming up. We're sisters. She cares. It's not that far-fetched, Doctor." She relaxed in her chair in an effort to look casual while she maintained perfect eye contact with me.

"I bet she cares a lot...an awful lot." I stared into her unblinking eyes.

Sydra leaned into me, fighting the space between us for dominance. She smiled with her mouth but tried to unlock me with her gaze. I had the upper hand this time, and she could feel the energy shifting in my favor. We were arm wrestling, and this time, I had her wrist bent towards the table ready for collapse. She tried to seem unshaken, but after her episode yesterday, I knew I could get her. She's fully aware that I knew she *could* come undone now, another strike against her. What's more, she knows she can come undone. My guess is that it's that fact which scares her the most. She's too fragile to keep her act up for long. I just have to wait her out, win the pissing contest.

"What is it you want Dr. Garris?" She pressed her luck, hoping I was here on a hunch that I had no theory for. "You're always spouting off about directness. What is your big revelation, sir? Stop raising the bet and just show me your cards. After all, it was you who said we don't have all the time in the world here."

"Ok. We'll play it this way." I leaned into the trench and looked her in her statuesque face, unafraid of her charms. "Your little game didn't work, Sydra. I know what you're hiding. I've found the holes you've purposefully left out of your story, and I know what you've done...or should I say what you *haven't* done. What I don't exactly know is why."

"Why what?" She didn't break her gaze.

"Why did you confess to the murder your sister committed?" I dropped the bomb.

She said nothing, only grinned on one side of her mouth and shook her head at me. She reclined again, trying too hard to relax her body language, a dead giveaway.

"Come on, Syd, why?" I teased her with the cadence of my voice, knowing it would etch her pretty teeth.

"I think you're the one who needs help, Doctor. You're quite the conspiracy theorist, aren't you?" She sounded cool, but I knew it wouldn't last.

"No. It's no theory. And you better start giving me some good answers, or you're both going to fry. If you're trying to act out in some guilt-ridden attempt at martyrdom, you're gonna fail miserably. You'll go down for nothing and take her with you. Two more lives down the drain just like that." I snapped my fingers sharply, slicing into the air in front of her stone face.

She sighed and looked at the wall for a few seconds, then back at me. She bit her bottom lip just enough to make it swell a bit, and somehow managed to fill the air with her sensuality in a matter of seconds. It wasn't the reaction I anticipated. I was more prepared for a breakdown styled similarly to the one yesterday. But no, she was too regimented today and was about to use the only weapon she had left. She was like an animal with the ability to cognitively release her pheromones. She knew I was on to her and was moving on to Plan B, releasing her scent for me to catch.

"I need this to work out for me, Doctor. There's plenty you don't know, and it frankly doesn't matter. I want to go to trial for this, and I want temporary insanity." She softened her voice and licked her lips so subtly I almost missed it. "There must be something we can work out. I'm an actress, and with that profession, comes a lot of different talents. I'm sure we can find one to suit your tastes."

I felt my entire body stiffen for just a moment. After all, Sydra Parramore had just made an official pass at me. It couldn't be swallowed easily. She stared at me in a way I hadn't been looked at in years, and she knew that for a split second, I wanted to take her deal.

However, I knew I couldn't give into her. If I did, then I would never have answers, and justice may never be done. The good doctor in me hushed the lonesome man, and I prepared for war. She'd just fired her first shot.

CHAPTER 24

SYDRA

$\mathcal{J}$ had to hand it to Peter Garris. He was no idiot, and certainly could not be easily swayed. I've met few men with his intellect and willpower in my life, maybe none. My attempt to deal with this situation was failing, and I could clearly see that. Somewhere along the way, a thread had been pulled, and the sweater would soon unravel if I didn't act quickly. Something I'd said had tipped him off. I didn't know if it was my panic attack, or if there was a hole somewhere, I hadn't found. None of that mattered anymore, however, because he knew the truth. He wasn't going to un-know it, and would never let it go. What was important now was that I win him over, and I intended to do it by any means necessary... which in my experience, usually meant one thing.

When I first asked him in my sexiest voice what could be done to remedy this situation, he said nothing in return. He just stared back at me with his mouth posed like he was going to speak, though he didn't make a sound. My guess is he was trying to find the will to resist, and I could respect that. He took his profession seriously enough, but at the end of the day, I also knew he was a man, and I was a famous actress. I'd have him doing what I wanted soon enough.

"Tell Miss Paramore how she can help," I said with narrowing bedroom eyes while I traced my bottom lip with my thumb.

"I'm not biting that line," he smiled, "so you can lose the act, right now, before I call one of the guards in. I'll be glad to share my opinions with them, as well as the judge, without your explanations if you'd like."

I felt my face redden with both embarrassment and anger and I had no rebuttal. I wasn't used to rejection of any kind, especially from men. I had no idea how to proceed and was suddenly very aware of my clothes and unwashed hair.

"You had better start shooting straight. I *have* figured this out, and I'm your only lifeline right now, Sydra. If I go to the powers at be right now and let them start digging, then you and your sister are gonna be up a creek while I'm on the bank with your life jackets. If I were you, I'd take serious advantage of my curiosity. You're both going to want as much sympathy and leniency as possible from wherever you can get it. You have no idea the plans being made for you from behind closed doors right now. So start singing." His patience was wearing thin, and I knew it.

"Can I at least get a smoke?" I said with relent hanging on my tongue. "It's been days, and I have the shakes something fierce."

"No...you do better spinning your little webs with

a cigarette in your hand. No tobacco. Just you and me, right here, right now," he said with his eyebrows arched into angry mountain peaks.

I fidgeted a little bit and rearranged myself in the uncomfortable chair. I looked towards the doctor but not directly at him, which I knew showed weakness. I also knew he was watching even my slightest movements, and could hear the things unspoken. I was shaken. He'd succeeded in getting to me. I could hear his battle song and was reluctantly surrendering my weapon while he waived his pretentious flag. He'd won.

"I don't know if I can give you every detail you want from me because I don't know if I have them all," I spat back because I was surrendering, both my will and my lies. If I could have lifted my chained hands higher, I would have thrown them into the air. "The truth is, there's a lot of grey. I have just started to become clear on what's black and white...and that's the damn truth."

"Sydra, it's ok if you've been genuinely confused. It's also ok if you don't have the best answers, as long as they're as true as you understand them to be. That being said, what *can* you give me to work with?" He readied his pen.

"What I can give you is a story that matters, and you can take that story and do with it whatever you have to." I leveled with him out of pure exhaustion.

"Ok, go ahead," he answered softly this time and relaxed his war stance.

"There was once a little girl who lived in a far away land, far away from any civilization, far away from anything beautiful. She was born to a mother one loaf of bread away from hooking and to a father with an IQ of 80 with a heart like pavement. Her Daddy ran off for good after getting out of prison and left the defected little girl and her mother all alone. Her mother, shocked at her seemingly good fortune, was then chosen to marry the king of all the land. He is the fast-talking town hero with golden hair and strapping good looks. He and the little girl's mother have another daughter, a princess with beauty so strong she needed nothing else to get by. She is doted over by all who pass her by. The newborn daughter is treated like the royalty she is, while her Daddy, the King, far past his prime, grows more bored and restless everyday. He looks to his step-daughter, the ugly duckling, satisfied that she isn't his own flesh and blood. He takes her as his favorite hobby when she is just eight years old, and his quiet queen allows it. He takes her hopes, dreams, and womanhood away, and she is now soiled to everyone in the kingdom. Meanwhile, the princess grows wickedly jealous of his attention to her non-royal sister and holds onto it for twenty years. She flees to find her happiness in other more exciting domains but comes up empty-handed. She eventually comes back to the small kingdom and disgustingly lures her father into her web, wanting the king for herself. Only, when she starts to get what she wants, she decides she doesn't want it anymore. The sister she's betrayed comes to her rescue and takes her pain away, slaying the king like the fire-breathing dragon he is. The princess then takes the sword from her sister's hand and repays her the only way she knows how." My voice had become a faint whisper by the end of the tale.

Dr. Garris passed me the handkerchief out of the pocket of his blazer to wipe the tears from my sunken face; they were the first truly genuine ones I'd cried in all this time. As he processed the things I'd said, I could tell he knew the truth was finally escaping from me and that the tears were just the secrets, lies, and hurt leaving my body. He had his answers.

After letting me cry a bit, he finally spoke. "Sydra. I see what is going on here....and though I feel for you and certainly for your sister, I cannot simply look the other way. We both have a responsibility to tell the truth and to uphold the law."

"And when we do?" I dabbed at my eyes.

Dr. Garris sighed, his eyes cast down a bit. "You will probably get a perjury charge, but that's a lot better than first-degree murder. It won't all just go away, but there is some light at the end of the tunnel, truly. And as for Jimmi-Lyn...she has a good shot at a defense plea. Given her history, a jury is likely to look at her favorably. She may be able to get off all together, but that'll be something she'll need to discuss with an attorney."

I sat with my body frozen as he spoke but managed to coax my lips to move again. "But see, there's something else that makes this extremely complicated, Dr. Garris. The princess in my little tale was a very naughty girl. When she came to town she also seduced the stable boy only a day before the king's passing...and she now carries a new prince or princess in her womb." I moved my hand to my stomach, resting it there.

"Sydra, are you saying that you're pregnant?" His eyes became huge.

"About two months along," I patted my belly, tearing up again.

CHAPTER 25

JIMMI-LYN

ᓀ wished we never had to leave the hidden tobacco field. I didn't care whose land it was, because, in my mind, it would always belong to Vanse and me. It would be our alternate universe where we go untouched by the rest of the world, and I would keep it with me forever. For a second, I closed my eyes and tried to transport myself back there, just in case it would work.

When the dark forced us to go, I picked a perfect maple leaf up off the ground and put it into my pocket so I could have a small piece of the place with me always. I needed something to cling to, on the off chance that I never made it back. I thought something that had lived in that special place its whole life might have some magic on it, and I could use some magic.

I climbed back into the cab of the truck, tucking the blanket we'd just been lying on as a couple, behind my back. Vanse hopped into the driver's seat and started the engine, which took two tries. Tony Bennett's voice seeped out of the fuzzy speakers and blended with the humming evening wind. I listened to him sing, "I'm wild again, beguiled again. Bewitched, bothered, and bewildered, am I." Then, I watched the night slowly creep into our special place like a lord reclaiming his sovereignty as we pulled away. I only looked back a few seconds, because if I had lingered, I might have stayed there forever. And, right now, I don't live in a world where that's possible.

Vanse reached down and turned the radio up a little bit. "I think we might have ourselves a song, J.L."

I scooted close to him and laid my head on his shoulder as we made our way back down the dirt road, our bodies as stirred up and jumping as the dust itself.

Vanse followed me into the house when we got back with no intention of going anywhere. He walked straight back to the bedroom and took his clothes off, piling them on top of my dresser. He pulled the covers back and plopped down on the cool floral sheets like he owned the place, which I loved. I leaned my head against the doorframe, smiling while I watched him. Leaving hadn't even occurred to him, and I think, maybe, my home was his now.

"What are you lookin' at? Get over here and snuggle me, girl." He playfully smacked the bed beside him.

I giggled like a schoolgirl and pulled my dress off over my head before I stepped out of my slip. I watched both items fall, loving how they crumpled up on the floor by Vanses' shoes. I didn't care that I was completely naked; I wanted him to see. I didn't try to hide. I just walked towards him, arms by my sides, until I crawled under the tattered patchwork quilt and laid my head down on the pillow facing him.

"I can't believe I'm here with you." I bit my bottom lip, smiling at him.

He pulled me in close and kissed me on the tip my nose. "I'll always be right here," he said before closing his eyes.

I laid my cheek down against his bare chest, feeling the scattered hair tickle my skin. I had what I'd always wanted...in the most bizarre possible timing.

I lied awake for hours, curled up in his arms while he slept effortlessly. I felt safe for the first time ever in that house, something I didn't believe was possible before tonight. It didn't matter what had happened here before, because tonight I decided that the pain and shame I'd felt belonged to someone else. I was a different girl then, and that was a different life. In this life I was nestled securely in the bend of Vanse's strong arm, feeling the heat from his body warm my own. I was okay.

The room was cool with the night air, and the bedroom window was cracked about two inches to coax the midnight breeze inside. The frogs hummed a simple lullaby for me from their mud holes, and I had found total peace in the arms of a man. That's another thing I never thought would happen for me, not in a million years. Nothing could ever change what Sid took away from me when I was younger, but now, as a woman, I realized Vanse gave me something greater than all that I lost. He'd given me redemption, and I was free.

While I lay there next to the love of my life, part of me wished we would just run away together when the sun came up. We would flee to some foreign country where no one knows our names, and we would leave the past whipping around in the Tobaccoville wind. But as much as I wanted that fantasy, and as content as I felt in one respect, another gnawing refused to leave me. I was finally vacant of Sid, but not of my sister.

Sydra moved about constantly in the back of my mind, though I'd tried so hard to ignore her all day long. I knew now, in the blackest part of the night, with only my soul and myself awake, that I had to do the right thing by her. It was my turn to redeem someone now. I knew it more than ever because I'd just had my own redemption. If I didn't step up, Sydra would never get hers. It was more than guilt driving me; it was responsibility.

As strongly as the selfish part of my heart beckoned me to run away from it all, the good part of it knew I couldn't let her take this fall for me. She wasn't well, and she needed help badly. I knew that there was something very wrong inside of her after talking to her this morning, though I'd put it out of my mind while I had my perfect day with Vanse. I told her I would think about how to proceed over the next day or two, but I had the answer already. I wouldn't continue with the lie any longer. I wouldn't let an ill woman sit in my place anymore, no matter the things she'd done in the past. It was wrong, and no matter how I tried, I couldn't rearrange it to make it right.

I gazed up at Vanse, whose breathing let me know he had drifted into his deepest sleep now. I loved him so very much, to the point it almost made me gutless. I loved him to the point I could almost let Sydra bear my burden. *Almost.* The problem was, I had a paramour myself. Sydra was my other love.

I would tell him in the morning that I'd chosen to turn myself in. Then, from there, I will pray. Maybe it's written somehow in the stars for the truth to set me free and then deliver me to his arms again. Just maybe I'm lucky enough to get handed that destiny along with this one.

I finally fell asleep with a clear conscience, knowing I was choosing to do the right thing, hoping to find blessings because of it. I also hoped Vanse would understand, and that need be, he would wait for me. In the meantime, I will hold onto this perfect day we had, letting it carry me as long as it has to. I will keep it close by....the memory, and of course, my maple leaf.

CHAPTER 26

SYDRA

"How long have you known you're pregnant, Sydra?" Dr. Garris threw his glasses down and pinched the aging area between his tired eyes. I'd completely exhausted yet another person of me.

"Not long at all," I responded. "I just recently realized it with everything that's been going on."

"Have you even taken a test? Or do you only suspect that you're pregnant?"

"I haven't taken a test, but I'm sure," I responded quietly, my eyes cast downward.

"If this is just a ploy to—"

"It isn't," I cut him off. "I'm sure. I wouldn't make something like this up. This isn't about me."

Dr. Garris sighed deeply and closed his eyes for a second before putting his glasses back on. He picked up my file, the one with the cigarette burn, and perused it for several minutes while we sat in silence. He flipped through page after page, huffing and shaking his head at certain points. I sat in silence, letting him do it. I didn't have it in me to play with him anymore. My pawns were all used up, and the king was in check. My eyes crossed when I tried to look at the board. It was over.

"Sydra, we'll get back to your *condition* in just a minute. First, I need to know," he said throwing the file on the table, "was everything you said just one big manipulation, or did you believe the lies you were spitting at me?"

"It was both." I answered honestly, "I did try to manipulate you, mainly so I could save my sister, but also in hopes of getting the easiest punishment for myself. You know that now, so there's no point in denying it anymore. My story was going to end with my father attacking Jimmi-Lyn, and me shooting him to defend her. I was hopefully going to get off on temporary insanity, or self-defense, if that worked. That was the grand lie I was waiting to reveal at the perfect moment. What happened is my sister rescued me, and in return, I've tried to do the same for her. In the middle of it all, I remembered things I'd blocked out, things I'd seen and changed somehow over the years. That's when I first panicked. It was like waking up out of a coma with no idea who you are anymore. Now, I know most of the facts...but am still fuzzy on a lot of the details. So, to answer you...it was both truth and lies...and I'm not sure I know the difference of all of them yet. I'm not sure if I will, or if this even makes any sense to you," I responded candidly and somberly.

"Sydra," Dr. Garris said my name gently, "I think I'm getting a clear picture of what's going on now. There's an entire school of thought that says the human mind can suppress difficult memories as a coping mechanism, which is what I believe you've done here. It's a relatively new idea in my field, and a lot of my colleagues reject it. I don't think you are insane or incapable of recovery, but I'm going to have to work hard to prove that. I will need your cooperation."

"Where do we go from here, Dr. Garris? Am I going to jail?"

"I don't know, Sydra." Dr. Garris tried not to look defeated.

"Am I going to an asylum?"

Dr. Garris didn't answer my question but instead responded with his own statement. "I'm going to need you to take a pregnancy test immediately. I also have a series of mental health tests I need you to take. Like I said, you have to be fully compliant with me now, Sydra."

"I understand." I nodded to him stoically.

"Ok," Dr. Garris stood up, leaving his pen and papers where they were. "I'm going to go talk to an officer and see about getting you your test right away. Stay put."

I looked at my feet that were chained to the stationary chair and held up my cuffed hands to him.

"Right. Sorry," he mumbled exiting the room, obviously exasperated.

When he walked out, I looked down at my slightly swollen belly and imagined the tiny infant living inside of it. I wondered if I were carrying a boy or a girl, wondered if it would look like Vanse or like me. I imagined it sleeping peacefully in there, in its seemingly perfect cocoon, with no idea what was going on, its world just outside. I couldn't help but think of how I'd already messed things up so badly for this child. How unfortunate it was that its little soul lived inside of me.

Discovering I was pregnant, along with my new-found memories had changed everything. I realized my life had been a sham I'd built for myself. I may be behind bars now, but I think I've been imprisoned all along. Yet, somehow, from that prison I was still able to damage people's lives irreparably....practically everyone I ever knew, all the way down to Dan McCreedy was destroyed because they crossed paths with me. They were flies all tangled up in my web that was so complex I didn't even know how to navigate it myself.

From behind my walls, I was able to send my mother to her deathbed knowing I hated her, was able to welcome Sid back into Jimmi-Lyn's life and was able to let Vanse knock me up. Now I was about to ruin the life of someone who hadn't even been born yet. Maybe I already had. Maybe just the fact that I'm half Sid, and that this baby is half me, had sealed its little fate. Maybe I'd already branded it and was starting the cycle all over again. I was either about to create a victim or a monster, and neither one was any way to live a life. At the end of the day, those two things are all I've ever been able to create, or to be.

I would make a terrible mother. I've tried to be Jimmi-Lyn's savior, and have failed miserably. The one good deed I've attempted in my entire life has just blown up in everyone's faces. I pulled the pin off the grenade myself and swore not to throw it. Now, here I have. I don't know what makes me think I won't do that to this baby.

No matter my intentions, I'll mess it up.

I rubbed my stomach and could feel the tears forming, not for myself, but for the infant. Maybe there was a way I could still spare this innocent child...and anyone else doomed to cross my path in the future, as well. There is still one scenario where I can finally be the hero instead of the victim. I have one option left to turn off the music we've all grown so accustomed to swaying to. I can stop it, that vicious pattern that's harvesting all our souls, one by one. I'll chop it at the very root this time, leaving no seeds scattered behind to grab the dirt again.

I tickled my lower belly and hummed *Rockabye Baby* quietly to myself, and let one last tear fall to the ground in the child's honor. I reached my cuffed hands out and grabbed Dr. Garris' pen that he'd left sitting on the table. I managed to get the sharper side turned around with my right hand, and aimed it at my pulsating left wrist.

I whispered, "God forgive me," under my weepy breath and began to dig the instrument into my exposed vein, evicting the Bumgarner blood from its lair.

CHAPTER 27

JIMMI-LYN

 woke up when the rays of light reached through the window and started playing with my eyelashes. For a moment I breathed in the scent of freshly cut grass sneaking through the screen, while I listened to what the birds were chattering about. It took me a good minute to remember myself, and what this morning meant. This was the morning I would tell Vanse what I had decided to do, and begin to face what my world would become. My stomach dropped to my ankles the moment I thought about it, but I'd simply have to pick it back up and press on. I'd made my decision.

I glanced at my nightstand, noticing my open day planner laying by my purse. It was July 4th. Until now, I'd completely forgotten the holiday. I never celebrated with anything more exciting than shooting off home-made fireworks in the field, but that would be better than the explosion about to come. Today I wasn't going to celebrate my independence; I was going to surrender it to the state of North Carolina.

Vanse lay beside me undisturbed, completely unknowing of what his day would soon become. I kissed him on the forehead and stroked his disheveled hair while I thought of what to say to him when he first opened his eyes. I don't think there is a good way to start a conversation that ends with me in jail today. I didn't know what to say, and what I dreaded most was the look I knew he'd have on his face when I finally found the words. I didn't want to be the cause of the pain I knew he was about to feel, but there was no way around it.

I was lost deep in my thoughts when the phone rang so abruptly that I almost jumped out of my skin. Vanse stirred slightly at the noise, but it didn't wake him. I scrambled to my feet and grabbed my thin nightshirt out of the bottom drawer of my nightstand, struggling to pull it on while I dashed to the kitchen. I was shaking slightly from both nerves and the chill of the morning and was half out of breath by the time I grabbed the receiver on the fifth ring.

"Hello?" I answered, clearing my throat, shivering harder when the cold Bakelite plastic pressed against my cheek.

"Hello, Ms. Brawley?" the voice on the other end asked with an even tone.

"Yes, that's me," I answered curiously, not recognizing the voice on the other end.

"This is Dr. Peter Garris with the University of Chapel Hill Department of Criminal Psychology. I've been handling your sister's psychological evaluation the past little while." The voice was all business, but not rude.

"Yes, sir," I answered then held my breath. *What did*

he want with me?

"I'm afraid I have some disturbing news about Ms. Bumgarner," he hesitated.

"What is it?" I could feel my heart pounding in my ears, and I broke an instant sweat.

"I'm sorry to have to be the one to share this with you, Ms. Brawley. Ms. Bumgarner was found in a semi-conscious state after what appeared to have been an attempt to take her life yesterday." He almost blurted the news, and I could tell he was nervous now.

"Dear God," I whispered, my eyes starting to fill up with tears. "How?"

"She got an ink pen and attempted to cut her wrist with it. I hate to be so graphic, Ma'am." I sensed sorrowfulness in his inflection, as if he felt somehow responsible.

"Oh my God." My speech was muffled with tears I didn't attempt to control.

"She was rushed to the infirmary where the staff was able to revive her. She is in serious but stable condition at the present time."

"I—I'm speechless," I whispered before wiping my sweaty hands on my shirt.

"I understand you came to visit Ms. Bumgarner yesterday. I just missed you and had an early morning conference with her myself just before the incident."

"Yes, sir," I answered, trying to catch my breath, still in a complete state of shock.

"Did she seem upset when you spoke to her?"

"Yes, she did," I admitted, wondering if my time to

start confessing was upon me. "She...she wasn't in the best place...mentally...when I saw her."

"I didn't think so either," he concurred, "and I had to try to make some decisions about what needs to happen as far as her care, and her impending trial."

"I see," I urged him to continue, my voice small and nervous.

"I was able to get in front of a judge late yesterday afternoon after things settled down somewhat. I hope it will be of some relief to you... As per my findings and suggestions, Ms. Bumgarner has been deemed incompetent of standing trial for the murder of Sid Bumgarner. It looks like she will spend a minimum of 3 years in a psychological institution, where she will get the help she needs. At that point, her eligibility for release will be examined. This is excellent news, all things considered, Ms. Brawley. Had she gone to trial, she was facing life in prison and knowing the North Carolina judicial system, possibly the death penalty. Though, I'm not sure she would have made it that far, especially after her attempt yesterday. I feel that the best place for her now is a mental facility."

I didn't respond for a moment. "I'm still in such shock, Doctor...I'm almost sick to my stomach. I'm sorry."

"That's quite understandable, Ma'am," he answered kindly. "Please, take all the time you need to, Ms. Brawley."

"What do think is wrong with my sister? Mentally, I mean? What exactly is it?" I asked.

"I believe your sister suffers from a very mild form

of Schizophrenia and a clinical level Narcissistic disorder. She seems to distort reality at times and needs to go through a treatment program first and foremost."

"What kind of treatment will she be given?" I hesitated. "I...I've heard some really bad stories about women in these...um...facilities. I don't mean to offend you. I just want to know. Is Sydra going to be on heavy sedatives? Will she receive shock treatment?" I was terrified, hearing my voice asking these things about my sister.

"Ms. Brawley, I won't lie to you. There are a lot of things that go on in the asylums that I do not agree with. I'm currently battling against my colleagues about such matters. However, I have an ally at the facility Sydra will be residing at. I cannot promise medications won't be used, but I can promise she will not be subjected to shock treatments or surgeries under my watch."

"I appreciate that, Doctor." I felt my muscles relax just a bit. "If she gets better will any charges be filed against her at that time? Could there still be the possibility of a trial occurring when she gets out of the psychiatric facility?"

"I'm going to try very hard to not let that happen, Ms. Brawley. There are ways for her to get the help she needs, recover, and still avoid charges being filed. Her attorney is working with the D.A. right now to strike a deal that's dependent upon her successfully completing her three years of treatment under my supervision. I think your sister's future looks good at this point. Most importantly, she is extremely compliant at the moment. They've started her on a few extremely mild medications to calm her down. She knows she needs help and seems happy to take it today. It looks like all parties are becoming satisfied, which means they are unlikely to go after her later. It is my opinion your sister will never face trial." His confidence filled me with at least some hope.

"Thank you, Dr. Garris, for the personal call. Thank you so very much. I appreciate everything you've done for my sister during this awful time." My mind raced, and I was filled with both grief and gratitude.

What he said had just changed everything. Sydra was going to a place she needed to go to work through her issues. If I confessed now, she could do time for perjury. All of this was clearly more than she could handle...and God only knows what my fate would be. I was still conflicted in some way, yet knew I'd gotten off scott free. I wasn't going to talk at this point. I couldn't see how that would benefit either one of us now.

"And Ms. Brawley," Dr. Garris continued when I thought the conversation was over, "I thought I would let you know that I am available for counseling sessions... and I'm legally required to be discrete if...if there's anything you'd like to work on together. If there's anything you need to talk about, I'm here, pro bono in your case." His voice sounded strange, and I got the impression he knew more about me than I'd realized. However, I felt safe, like if he did know anything, maybe he was on my side.

"Thank you, Dr. Garris. I'll definitely consider that... um, will I be able to see Sydra at any point before she's moved, or during her recovery? I'm obviously worried sick about her."

"I'm afraid Ms. Bumgarner will not be permitted visitors during the beginning phases of her treatment, which is starting as soon as all the paperwork is filed. However, Ms. Brawley, we will need you again...in about seven months your presence will be requested." The doctor's voice sounded suddenly strange and cautious.

"Oh? Another hearing of some sort?" I furrowed my brow trying to read between the lines.

"No...no, nothing like that. Are you sitting down, Ms. Brawley?"

I lowered myself into a kitchen chair, abruptly nervous again. "Yes, sir."

"I have one last thing to share with you. I'm afraid I'm not sure how to tell you this, so excuse me for being the one to lay so much on you this morning. Your sister asked me to speak to you about it on her behalf. It seems Ms. Bumgarner is currently with child...approximately eight weeks into her gestation."

Silence.

"She would have conceived close to the time of the initial incident, though she's made no mention of the child's father," Dr. Garris spoke as though he were tip-toeing for my sake, "and Ms. Bumgarner has requested that you accept custody of the baby upon her giving birth. This is something you can decline. However, if you choose to do so, the infant will be awarded to the guardianship of the State of North Carolina, and eventually put up for adoption. I want you to know you have the right to refuse, and that it is in no way your personal or legal responsibility to take this on, Ms. Brawley. The choice is 100% yours to make." He paused for my response.

I sat with my bony hand clasped tightly over my mouth. I was completely shocked by the revelation and didn't know what to say. Now my sister, who had attempted to take her own life, was *pregnant*? I felt short of breath for a few seconds and had no idea how to react.

It still sickened me to my core knowing Sydra had ever been with Vanse, who obviously had fathered this baby. He was the love of my life, and I couldn't stand the thought of him so much as touching her. My guess is she knew this, which is why she didn't disclose his name. Maybe she thought she was sparing my feelings somehow. Or, maybe, she was worried Vanse would have nothing to do with the baby. Would either of us want this kind of reminder of Sydra and the murder in our lives every day?

On the one hand, I thought it would be completely unhealthy for me to spend every waking day with this child - Sid Bumgarner's lineage. But, on the other hand, it's an innocent baby. It's biologically related to me, and something I would never be able to give myself. The baby's mother had tried to *kill* herself while carrying it. And I am madly in love with this child's natural father, a man who would make an incredible Daddy. How could I not do the right thing by all of us?

"Are you there, Ms. Brawley?" Dr. Garris' voice

brought me back to reality.

"Yes, yes, I'm sorry. I'm a bit shocked...again." I laughed awkwardly, "This has all been so much to process at once." I answered, swallowing hard.

"Completely reasonable, Ms. Brawley. I've put a lot on your breakfast plate this morning," he replied.

"Um...I...who will notify me when it's time for the delivery?" I stumbled through my response.

"That will be the institution, Ms. Brawley, if you choose to accept Ms. Bumgarner's request."

"Yes, yes, of course. I-I don't want the baby ending up with strangers or orphaned. I...I accept...."

"Are you certain?" Dr. Garris confirmed.

"Yes, I'm sure," I answered knowing I wasn't quite sure but trying to go with my gut.

"You can expect some paperwork soon. I won't be handling the adoption. Ms. Bumgarner just wanted me to share this news with you initially. And please remember, as I said, my door is always open for you."

"Yes, sir. Thank you, Dr. Garris, for everything you've done for my sister. Take Care," I answered, truly grateful to him.

I slowly hung up the phone and rose to my shaky feet. I knew this morning would hold a ton of surprises, but they were vastly different than I could have ever imagined. I was not going to jail, and neither was Sydra. It was a terrible thing that led to this outcome, but I was thanking God they found her in time, and she'd be getting help.

The craziest part of it all was that it looked like we

were both about to be someone's mother...one by nature, and one by choice. There was going to be a new life, part of Vanse, of Sydra, and, even of me. I could hardly believe it...*me, a mother.*

My thoughts were interrupted by the sound of feet hitting the hardwood floor. Vanse had stirred and met me around the corner where the hall merges with the kitchen. He leaned against the wall shirtless, still wiping the sleep from his eyes, and smiled at me.

"Morning, pretty girl," he kissed my cheek while I stood frozen.

"We need to talk. Why don't you have a seat." I let out a nervous chuckle and took a deep breath.

"Ok." He lowered himself to the chair I had just been sitting in. "You sound awful serious so bright and early."

I walked to the window over the sink and cracked it for some fresh air before I started to speak. The wind rushed immediately inside with a smell slightly different than it had yesterday, a smell with less honey and more hay. It reminded me that summer was peaking and that Fall was just around the corner. I noticed the farmers were out readying the lush, ripe tobacco that had grown so tall in a matter of weeks. I could smell the prelude to the harvest, and I turned around to face Vanse.

"What is it, Pretty Girl?" He squinted into the sunlight that was beaming off of the scuffed up table.

"A new season."

EPILOGUE

SYDRA

$\mathcal{J}$ spent exactly three years and no more at Broughton Hospital in Morganton, North Carolina. The media went absolutely crazy when everything got out. They practically beat down the doors of the hospital, but couldn't ever get a glimpse of me on the inside. The world was shocked that Sydra Parramore had been committed to a psych ward.

I did my 36 months, talked to a lot of men in white coats, and swallowed a lot of horse pills. Luckily, my pregnancy, and Dr. Garris' adamant protesting, kept the stir stick out of my frontal lobe. I learned about a man named Rathburn, who'd so badly wanted to make me his Hollywood face of the Transorbital Lobotomy. When he didn't get his way, he finally retired, and the Criminal Psychology Department at Chapel Hill got a new director, one with all kinds of "new thinking". His ally at the Morganton facility took great care of his patient while his new position busied him.

After my three-year tenure was over, there was a whole new crop of gorgeous models decorating the newsstands. When I left Broughton, I didn't hear a peep from anyone. There wasn't a reporter or camera within a hundred miles of the tiny mountain town. No one cared about Sydra Parramore now, which was good, because she didn't really exist anymore. She died that day in Raleigh, and the body was resurrected as someone else entirely. Her image lingered for just a while longer, but there was no hair dye in insane asylums. The last bit of her faded away about six months in. I waved goodbye to the Hollywood starlet and knew she would never be back.

I used my time in lockup to get better. For a long time, I hadn't even realized I was sick. It was true what Dr. Garris said, though. I was a narcissist and a delusional one at that. Now I knew what I was, and the mostly brunette Sydra with a last name still to be determined will fight for life.

I deserved the years I got in Morganton. I didn't pull the trigger, but I killed my father when I brought him back into that house. I didn't touch my sister, but I hurt her too many times to try and count with every smug look, every ignored cry for help, and every cheap trick to pull Vanse away. I was guilty of many crimes I committed from a safe distance. I tried to end my life to atone for it all. I didn't want to get better because I didn't think I could. I thought the poison was in me, incurable, and would never leave my blood. I almost ended my bloodline altogether for that reason. I almost took two lives, and thought by doing so that I would save us both.

However, when I held my own 6 pound 12 ounce, blonde-headed, blue-eyed baby girl, I realized she'd save our lives. I knew I had to get better for her sake. In the five minutes I was given with her, my world changed completely. When I heard her cry, I knew I would do anything, or be anything for her. I kept her gorgeous newborn photo by my bed every day and promised her that she'd have a beautiful life.

After I had gotten out, I spent six months in a halfway house before buying an old car and renting a small cottage on a lake outside of Charlotte. I thankfully still had movie royalties coming in but was also helped by my old friend in Chapel Hill. He got me a job tucked away in an office far from the public eye where I quietly file tax returns from nine to five. My life looks very different than it did a few short years ago, and I've done it for *her*.

Once I felt like I had my bearings again, I got the guts to do the only thing I'd been thinking about for what was now closer to four years than three. Everything I'd done had been for the child, whose name I don't even know. Sometimes, to myself, I call her *Angel*. That's exactly what she'd been, and I know I wouldn't be alive right now if I hadn't seen her sweet face; the one with my turned up nose and her father's cobalt eyes.

I called the operator to find Jimmi-Lyn's address. She'd written me before my release saying she'd had the old house flattened and sold the field to the R.J. Reynolds Tobacco Company for a nice penny, some of which she'd sat aside for my angel girl. I wasn't surprised when I found no listing for a Jimmi-Lyn Brawley. Though she'd never told me anything in person, nor in a letter - in her effort to spare me emotionally, I had the feeling I wouldn't find her under that listing. Vanse and Jimmi-Lyn Newland, however, were listed twice in Thomasville, North Carolina. One was a personal listing and the other a handmade furniture store.

I drove the two hours from my place to Thomasville on a Thursday afternoon. I did my best to look nice. I wore a silk off-white shirt and an A-line linen skirt. I wore flats and pinned my naturally dish-water blonde hair back. I put on a little bit of pink lipstick, but nothing more. I wanted to look like someone's mother now, not someone's trophy. I didn't want to look anything like Sydra Parramore.

I could feel my hands growing sweatier and sweatier as I neared the address from the listing. My breath quickened, and for a moment I thought I would hyperventilate. Instead, I found myself in a driveway in front of a two-story white farmhouse with a wrap-around porch and dainty screen door. I reached for the handle of the car door when I heard a squeal in the distance. I looked around and couldn't see where it was coming from.

I stepped out of the car and walked onto the porch. When I got to the edge, I could see over a fence into the backyard. The most beautiful creature I'd ever seen, in her little white dress with sunflowers stitched on the hem, was being pushed back and forth on a tire swing, between Vanse and Jimmi-Lyn.

"Ok, one more time!" I heard Vanse shout, his voice sending chills up my arms.

"Weeeeee!" The little girl squealed before flying

into Jimmi-Lyn's arms.

"That was fun, Mommy!" she shouted out in the sweetest little southern drawl.

"Alright, now, let's get washed up for dinner." Jimmi-Lyn took the little girl by the hand and kissed her on top of her head in between her pigtails. "Come on, Faith."

They'd named her, *Faith*. It was perfect. Tears filled my eyes and I began to back away, blowing the little girl a kiss she'd never see. I hoped it would float through the air somehow and land on her chubby little cheek. Maybe she'd feel a tickle, and reach up and touch it. The love I had for her overwhelmed me. I knew then that the promise I'd made to her picture from day one had been kept. She was having a beautiful life.

I crept back into my car and pulled away as quietly as I could. I looked only briefly in my rearview mirror at the gorgeous southern summer sun setting behind me and allowed myself to smile for Faith. When I made it back to the highway, I started passing the endless rows of tobacco fields, each growing darker by the minute in the evening dusk. I couldn't help but remember something completely random I'd heard an old farmer say once when I was a child. I don't know his name or why he was speaking to me; I just remember playing by the field when he stopped and pointed at the ripe crops.

"Time to cure 'em. They've been brought up just right. Now I just gotta age 'em without changing their atmosphere too much. If it changes even a little, it could kill 'em all. Climate is everything, little girl. You remember that."

Climate is everything.

TOBACCO SUN

ACKNOWLEDGEMENTS

First I'd like to thank God for all of my blessings, and for making me a writer. Thank you for your divine wisdom, and plans for "a hope and a future" for me. Secondly, I thank my husband, Kimsey Hollifield, for always believing in me, supporting me, and rolling with my whims. I thank him for not trying to wash the dreamer out of me and for not thinking I'm nuts. *We* did it, babe!

Jack Lovingood, and Jennifer Hensley, you could not have better prepared me for this journey. When God gave me parents, he chose an artful father and an unyielding mother; and this book certainly wouldn't be here without either of those.

To Katie Sullivan, I am forever grateful. My fellow LowCountry writer read through the earliest drafts and never failed to build me up. She's a true gem, trench mate and wonderful writer. Thanks for giving me a chance before anyone else did. To Rick Pascocello, thanks for mentoring me, and showing me ways to make the manuscript sparkle. You gave me the confidence to try *harder*. To Mary Alice Monroe, I cannot appreciate your endorsement enough. You've been a warm and encouraging presence from the first time we met! I hope to earn my success with the talent and humble nature in which you earned yours. To sit on a shelf next to you is a great joy, and dream come true (thanks to Angela May for connecting us)!

A shout out to a few former teachers who have made all the difference: Carmen Murray, you were the first to call me an author on a first-grade report card...it stuck. To the late Jerdee Simpson, my third-grade teacher, thank you for letting me write stories in class even when I was supposed to be doing something else! Finally, a big thanks to Hollie McKinney, my high school English teacher, and cheerleading coach. You always made me feel like I shined, and I want you to know that your effort mattered.

Thank you to Joe and Jane Lanford for getting my husband a job in Winston-Salem, and making us a lot of dinners early in our marriage. Without this time period in the piedmont, Tobacco Sun would never have been born.

Last but far from least, a huge thanks to Pen Name Publishing. I couldn't be more grateful for Dionne Abouelela and the entire PNP family. You all made this book happen, and put your faith in a young southern writer with a big fat dream! There are not enough words.

My apologies if any names were left out. I truly thank every friend and family member from the bottom of my heart. A lot of people have been cheering me one for a long time, and I love you all!

ABOUT THE AUTHOR

 Lorna Hollifield was born in Asheville, North Carolina, but now enjoys the island life outside of Charleston, South Carolina with her husband, Kimsey, and two mutts, Scarlet and Daisy.

She's been an author from the time she could speak, always spinning yarns for anyone who would listen. She began her professional writing journey as a tourism and travel blogger, before finally deciding to pursue her dream of publishing fiction. Tobacco Sun is her first novel, and she's delighted to share it with the world! Discover more about Lorna at lornahollifield. com.

DID YOU LOVE THIS BOOK?

One of the best ways to support authors is by leaving a review. Reviews help with search engine ratings, retailer rankings, visibility, and they help readers like yourself find their next favorite book.

If you loved this title, you can leave your review on any retailers website, or on book discovery websites like GoodReads.

To share your Instagram photo, blog review, or YouTube video with us, you can find us on all social media:
Instagram: @PenNamePublishing
Twitter: @PenNamePublish
YouTube: @Pen Name Publishing
Facebook: facebook.com/pennamepublishing

CPSIA information can be obtained
at www.ICGtesting.com
Printed in the USA
FFOW05n0224260517